SILENT BATTLES

A Doctor's Journey in the World's Highest Battlefield

CHAITANYA VARMA

INDIA • SINGAPORE • MALAYSIA

Copyright © Chaitanya Varma 2025
All Rights Reserved.

ISBN
Paperback 979-8-89673-709-4
Hardcase 979-8-89699-311-7

Dedication

To my mom and dad, who have always stood by me, and to the soldiers who have suffered in silence and sacrifice

TABLE OF CONTENTS

Chapter 1

A YEAR IN PARADISE

The Call to Adventure

The call to adventure doesn't often come with dramatic fanfare; in real life, it arrives quietly, weaving itself into the fabric of daily routine until its presence is undeniable. For Arjun, that day arrived in an understated way, on a typical Srinagar morning—a crisp breeze off Dal Lake, the sun still half-hidden behind the Zabarwan Range. The thin air carried the earthy scent of fallen Chinar leaves, and the distant murmur of hospital activity drifted through the open windows of his quarters. There was no sudden decision, just a growing restlessness, the call taking root in the back of his mind, slowly demanding his attention.

He had lived in this city for a year now. A year, but it felt both a lifetime and a fleeting moment.

"Yaar, how can you still be thinking about Siachen?" Captain Shashank's voice cut through his reverie. Standing in the doorway of their quarters, hands shoved deep into the pockets of his olive-green jacket, Shashank raised an eyebrow. "We've got it made here, Arjun. Good food, great company, and no frostbite! What more do you want?"

Arjun chuckled, tossing the paperback he'd been pretending to read onto his bunk. "You sound like someone already planning his retirement, Shashank."

Shashank laughed, the sound deep and resonant, bouncing off the walls. "Retirement's a long way off, my friend. But I'm definitely not volunteering for Siachen. That place breaks people."

Arjun knew his friend was half-joking, but there was truth there. Siachen was legendary in the army, and not in the romanticised way that civilian life sometimes painted it. Temperatures that could kill faster than bullets, terrain that punished every step, and isolation that weighed on even the toughest minds—it was no place anyone actively wished to serve.

Yet for months, the glacier had lingered in Arjun's thoughts, a distant call that grew louder every day.

"You know it's not about wanting to go," he said, sitting up. "It's about the challenge. Testing yourself in ways you can't anywhere else."

Shashank's expression softened, a flicker of concern crossing his face. "You think Siachen's some kind of test? You think you'll come back a hero, like in those novels you read? Arjun, people die out there. And it's not the bullets that get you—it's the cold, the altitude. It kills slowly, quietly. Don't romanticise it."

Arjun fell silent. Shashank's words were true; he'd read the reports, heard the stories from veterans who'd faced the glacier. Siachen was no Kashmir valley, no poetic retreat into the mountains. It was a battleground against nature itself.

But even so, the pull remained—a call he couldn't shake, growing louder with each passing day.

The Allure of Srinagar

It's hard to describe what makes Srinagar so intoxicating. Maybe it's the way the mountains seem to cradle the city, or the way the Dal Lake changes its personality depending on the time of day—serene and glassy in the mornings, bustling with life and shikaras in the evenings, and mysterious under the moonlight. Perhaps it was the people—the shopkeepers in the bazaars, the boatmen on the lake, and the warmth they showed despite the cold that often permeated the air.

The 92 Base Hospital, though functional and barebones, had become a sanctuary for Arjun. He remembered his first day—walking into the sprawling campus, a mix of old military buildings and newer structures, all set against the valley's backdrop. He was a nervous young captain, fresh out of medical school, and stepping into a world where life and death often danced on a razor's edge.

His quarters were a modest house shared with four other officers—his comrades, his friends. Each of them had their own room, and while the accommodations were basic, they were comfortable enough. His small window overlooked the hospital grounds, offering a glimpse of the Chinar trees and the ever-present mountains beyond.

Over the past year, Arjun had grown close to his roommates. Captain Shashank was the life of the room, always quick with a joke or a story, and his laugh was infectious. Captain Raghav, on the other hand, was quiet and introspective, a man of few words but deep thoughts. His eyes would often linger on the distant horizon, as if searching for something beyond the mountains.

Then there was Captain Mintu, who had become notorious for his pranks. He had a mischievous streak that kept them all on their toes. One morning he locked Shashank out of the room after morning showers, making him late for the briefing for which Shashank had to go on an exercise in Pokhran as a punishment.

Finally, Major Prasenjit. He was the oldest among them, a surgeonwho had seen more of the world than the rest combined. He rarely spoke about his time in Siachen, but when he did, they all listened. His stories were stark, devoid of embellishment, and each one carried the weight of his experiences. Arjun respected Prasenjit deeply, not just for his skill as a doctor, but for the quiet strength he exuded.

"Still thinking about it, aren't you?" Prasenjit's voice sliced through Arjun's thoughts as he entered the room in the fading light of evening.

"Thinking about what?" Arjun asked, though he knew perfectly well.

"Siachen," Prasenjit replied, his tone calm but direct. "It's not something you should take lightly, Arjun."

Arjun sighed, running a hand through his hair. "I know it's dangerous, Prasenjit. But... I don't know. I feel like I need to go. Like there's something I need to prove."

"To whom?" Prasenjit asked, settling onto the edge of his bunk, his dark eyes fixed on Arjun. He was silent for a moment, as though choosing his words carefully. "You've got nothing to prove, Arjun. Not to the army, not to any of us, and certainly not to yourself."

Arjun looked away, unsure of how to explain the restlessness that had been gnawing at him for months. Prasenjit had always had a way of seeing through him, much like Zoya Wani. Somehow, they both seemed to understand him more deeply than he understood himself.

But there was a pull—one that no words could dismiss.

Zoya Wani's Realm

Zoya Wani and Arjun had fallen into a comfortable routine over the past year. She worked as a civilian liaison officer at the hospital, and they would often steal moments together between shifts or during their off days. Their relationship had grown quietly, without fanfare or declarations, but it had become something solid, something Arjun had come to rely on.

One of their favourite spots was Nishat Bagh, one of the Mughal gardens overlooking Dal Lake. They would sit on the stone steps, sipping kahwa from thermoses, watching the sun dip below the horizon.

That evening, as they sat together, Zoya rested her head on his shoulder, her long hair falling softly around them like a curtain.

"Arjun," she said, her voice a soft whisper, "you've been different lately."

"Different how?" Arjun asked, though he had a feeling he knew where the conversation was heading.

"Quieter. More… distant." She lifted her head to look at him, her hazel eyes searching his. "I know you've been thinking about Siachen."

He exhaled slowly, his breath mingling with the cool air. "I have."

Zoya was silent for a moment, her gaze dropping to the lake below them. The shikaras were still gliding across the water, their passengers bundled up against the evening chill.

"I know you, Arjun," she said finally, her voice barely above a whisper. "You're not content here. You've never been content with… staying in one place. But Siachen… it's dangerous. I've seen the reports. I've talked to the soldiers who've come back. It's not another posting."

"I know," Arjun said quietly. "I'm not doing this because I want to leave. I'm doing it because… because it feels like the right thing to do. Like it's my duty."

Zoya's eyes filled with unshed tears, and she turned away, wiping them quickly. "Duty." She repeated the word as though it was an old, familiar wound. "And what about us?"

The question hung in the air between them, heavy and unavoidable. Arjun could hear the emotion in her voice, the fear beneath the calm facade. Zoya had always been strong, independent, and practical. But this was different. This wasn't a question about where they'd have dinner or what their next adventure in Srinagar might be. This was about something far more uncertain—their future.

"I'm not leaving you," Arjun said softly. "This isn't about running away or abandoning what we have. You mean everything to me." His voice softened, barely audible above the whispers of the evening breeze. "But I have to do this."

She didn't pull away, but her eyes searched his, as if trying to find a reason not to be afraid, not to feel like she was losing him.

"Why?" she asked, her voice breaking slightly. "Why do you have to go? You've already given so much, Arjun. You're a doctor. You save lives here every day. Isn't that enough?"

Arjun looked away, unsure of how to explain the gnawing feeling inside him, the restlessness that had grown over the past year. "I wish I could explain it better. It's… something inside me. Every time I hear about Siachen, every time someone talks about it, I feel this pull. Like I need to go. Like I need to be there."

Zoya shook her head, blinking back more tears. "That's not an answer, Arjun. That's you wanting to prove something to yourself. But what about us? What about the life we're building here?"

Arjun swallowed hard. She was right. It was selfish, in a way. He hadn't fully considered the impact this would have on her, on them. For him, Siachen was a test of endurance, a challenge, and once overcome, it would leave him stronger, more capable. But for her, it was something else entirely—a potential goodbye, a separation that could last for months, or worse, might never end.

The Rhythm of the Hospital

Life at the hospital continued as usual, though the weight of Arjun's decision to volunteer for Siachen loomed over him. The other officers would have something to say, no doubt, but he wasn't ready for their reactions yet. He needed to process his decision fully before facing the barrage of opinions that would surely follow.

At the hospital, things had been relatively quiet. The routine cases flowed in—altitude sickness, respiratory problems, and minor injuries from training exercises in the mountains. But every so often, there were reminders of the conflict raging beyond the valley's beauty. Soldiers came in with wounds from skirmishes along the Line of Control, their injuries sometimes more psychological than physical.

One morning, Arjun was in the middle of a routine examination when he was called to the trauma ward. A young soldier, no older than twenty-two, had been brought in with a gunshot wound to the leg. He had been on patrol near Kupwara when they were ambushed by militants. The bullet had lodged itself dangerously close to his femoral artery, and the immediate concern was stopping the bleeding.

Arjun scrubbed in quickly and joined Dr. Prasenjit in the operating room. The atmosphere was tense, but there was a practised calm to Prasenjit's movements as he gave instructions to the team. Arjun could feel his heart racing in his chest, but he followed Prasenjit's lead, assisting him as they worked to stabilise the soldier.

"He's young," Prasenjit muttered as he examined the wound more closely. "Too young for this."

Arjun nodded, focusing on his task. They worked in silence for hours, and eventually, they managed to remove the bullet and stop the bleeding. As they finished closing the wound, Arjun glanced at the young soldier's face—pale, unconscious, but alive.

When the surgery was over and the soldier was moved to the post-operative ward, Arjun stepped outside to catch his breath. The adrenaline of the operation was still coursing through him, but there was also a lingering sense of frustration. This young man had barely begun his life, and yet here he was, already marked by violence and conflict.

Prasenjit joined him outside a few minutes later, wiping his hands on a towel. He stood beside Arjun in silence for a moment, then spoke quietly. "You know, every time I see something like that, I'm reminded of how lucky we are. That we get to save lives."

"Yeah," Arjun agreed, though his mind was elsewhere.

Prasenjit glanced at him, clearly reading the tension in his posture. "You're still thinking about it, aren't you? Siachen?"

Arjun sighed, leaning against the railing. "I can't stop thinking about it."

Prasenjit was quiet for a moment, and when he finally spoke, his voice was softer. "Arjun, I've been there. I know what it is. And I won't lie to you—it's tough. Tougher than anything you've faced here. But I also understand why you feel you need to go."

Arjun looked at him, surprised by the admission.

"You're young," Prasenjit continued. "You still feel like you need to prove something to yourself, to the world. And maybe you do. But know that it's not all glory up there. There's a reason people come back changed. Some don't come back at all."

Arjun swallowed hard, the weight of his words sinking in. "I know it's dangerous. I'm not going into this lightly."

Prasenjit nodded, folding his arms across his chest. "I believe you. But remember, there's more to life than testing your limits. Don't lose sight of the people you leave behind."

Arjun thought of Zoya, her tear-filled eyes as she begged him not to make promises he couldn't keep. Prasenjit's words hit closer to home than he wanted to admit.

Comrades in Quarters

Later that evening, back at their quarters, the usual chaos reigned. Shashank was sprawled out on his bunk, flipping through an old magazine, while Mintu was busy playing cards with Captain Raghav, who wore his usual unreadable expression. The room smelled of dinner—something spicy, probably Mintu's doing, as he had a knack for sneaking extra chili into the mess food.

"Oi, Arjun!" Shashank called out as Arjun entered the room. "Where've you been? Saving lives again?"

"Something like that," Arjun muttered, dropping his bag onto his bunk.

"Come on, sit down," Mintu said, patting the empty chair beside him. "Join the game. Raghav's winning, and it's killing me."

Arjun smiled, though his mind was still on everything Prasenjit had said earlier. He sat down, trying to force himself to focus on the game, but it wasn't long before Raghav's keen eyes noticed his distraction.

"Alright, what's up with you?" he asked, tossing his cards onto the table in defeat. "You've been all quiet lately. That's not you."

Shashank sat up, raising an eyebrow. "Yeah, you've been acting strange. Come on, spill it. What's going on?"

Arjun hesitated, glancing around the room at his friends. He knew this was the moment he had been dreading—the moment he would have to tell them the truth. Taking a deep breath, he leaned forward and said, "I volunteered for Siachen."

The room went dead silent. Mintu's eyes widened in disbelief, and Raghav stopped shuffling the deck of cards in his hands. Shashank, who was usually quick with a sarcastic remark, stared at Arjun as if he had announced he was quitting the army.

"You did what?" Shashank finally said, his voice louder than usual. "You volunteered for Siachen? Are you out of your mind?"

Mintu shook his head, leaning back in his chair. "Man, I thought you were smarter than this."

Even Raghav, who rarely showed much emotion, looked genuinely concerned. "Siachen's not a joke, Arjun. Why would you want to go there?"

"I know it's dangerous," Arjun said, holding up his hands in defence. "But I've been thinking about it for months now. It's not about wanting to go—it's about needing to. I feel like it's something I have to do."

Shashank groaned, standing up and pacing the room. "You have to do it? Come on, man. There's nothing romantic about freezing your ass off on a glacier."

"It's not about romance, Shashank. It's about duty," Arjun said, trying to keep his voice steady. "I need to challenge myself. I need to—"

"You don't need to do anything," Shashank interrupted, his voice sharp. "You're already doing your duty right here. You're saving lives every day. Isn't that enough?"

Arjun didn't have an answer for him, not one that would make sense to anyone but him. The room had gone tense, and he could feel the weight of their stares pressing down on him. They were his closest friends, his brothers in arms, and yet, in this moment, it felt like he was on the outside looking in.

Shashank finally stopped pacing and turned to face him. "Arjun, you don't need to prove anything to anyone. You're a damn good doctor, and we're lucky to have you here. But Siachen? That's a different world, man."

Arjun ran a hand through his hair, feeling the frustration bubbling up inside him. "I'm not doing this to prove something. I—" He paused, searching for the right words. "I feel like I'm too comfortable here. Like I haven't been tested. I need to push myself, to see what I'm capable of."

Mintu, ever the prankster, was uncharacteristically serious as he leaned forward, resting his elbows on the table. "There are other ways to push yourself, Arjun. You don't need to go to the most dangerous place on earth to figure out who you are."

Raghav, who had been quiet up until now, finally spoke. His voice was soft, but his words cut through the room like a knife. "Are you sure this isn't about running away?"

Arjun blinked, caught off guard by the question. "Running away from what?"

Raghav shrugged, his dark eyes studying Arjun carefully. "I don't know. From Zoya? From whatever's going on in your head? Sometimes, when people make decisions like this, it's not about where they're going—it's about whether they're trying to escape."

The silence that followed was deafening. Arjun hadn't expected Raghav to say something so direct, but he wasn't wrong. The thought had crossed Arjun's mind more than once. Was he running away? Was this decision about escaping the life he had built here, the relationship that was growing more serious by the day? Or was it truly about the challenge, the duty he felt as an officer?

"I'm not running away," Arjun said, though the words felt heavy on his tongue. "I… I need to do this. For myself."

Shashank sighed, shaking his head. "You're going to do what you want, I know. Just promise me you'll be smart about it. Don't let some romantic notion of heroism get you killed out there."

Arjun nodded, though he could see the disappointment in his friends' eyes. They didn't understand, and maybe they never would. But he wasn't asking for their approval. He needed them to accept his decision, and in their own way, he knew they did.

Zoya's Silence

The days after that conversation passed in a blur of routine. The hospital was busy, and between shifts and the occasional emergency case, Arjun had little time to dwell on the fact that he was only a few days away from leaving Srinagar. But as the date of his departure grew closer, Arjun could feel the tension building inside him. Not because of Siachen, but because of Zoya.

She had been distant ever since that night in the garden, and he hadn't known how to fix it. They still saw each other at the hospital, shared brief moments in passing, but the warmth that had always been there between them felt strained. He knew she was struggling with his decision, and he didn't blame her. But it was harder than he'd anticipated to see the way it was affecting her—affecting them.

One evening, he found her sitting on a bench near the hospital grounds, staring out at the Chinar trees, her face a mask of quiet contemplation. The sun was setting, casting a warm, golden light over the landscape, but there was a chill in the air that seemed to mirror the distance growing between them.

Arjun approached slowly, unsure of how to start the conversation. "Zoya?"

She looked up at him, her expression unreadable. "Hi," she said, her voice soft but guarded.

He sat down beside her, the silence stretching between them. For a long moment, neither of them said anything. He wasn't sure how to bridge the gap that had formed, but he knew he couldn't leave things like this.

"Zoya, I—"

"Don't," she interrupted, her voice quiet but firm. "Don't say you're sorry. Because I know you're not."

Arjun closed his mouth, the words dying on his lips. She was right. He wasn't sorry for his decision, even though he hated what it was doing to them.

"I've been trying to understand, Arjun," she continued, her gaze fixed on the horizon. "I've been trying to make sense of why you feel like you have to do this. But no matter how much I think about it, I can't. I can't make sense of why you'd leave everything behind—leave me behind—for something that could take you away forever."

Her words hit him like a punch to the gut, and he struggled to find a response. "I'm not leaving you behind, Zoya. I'm coming back."

She let out a bitter laugh, shaking her head. "You can't promise that, Arjun. You can't look me in the eye and say for sure that you'll come back. How many stories have I heard? Siachen is unforgiving. People die up there, Arjun. Good people. And I can't... I can't sit here and pretend everything's going to be fine when I know the risks."

Arjun reached for her hand, but she pulled away, standing up abruptly. "I'm not angry at you for wanting to go. I'm angry because you don't see what you're leaving behind."

He stood up as well, his chest tight with frustration and guilt. "I do see what I'm leaving behind, Zoya. I see you. I know this isn't fair, and I know it's hard. But this is who I am. I signed up for this. You knew that when we started this relationship."

Her eyes filled with tears, and she looked away, blinking them back. "I didn't sign up for this, Arjun. I didn't sign up to fall in love with someone who might not come back."

The air seemed to leave his lungs at her words. She had never said it out loud before—neither of them had. Love. It hung between them now, raw and unspoken until this moment, and Arjun could feel the weight of it pressing down on his chest.

"Zoya…" he began, his voice faltering.

But she shook her head, stepping back. "Don't. Just… don't make this harder than it already is."

For a moment, he stood there, unsure of what to do or say. Part of him wanted to tell her that he wouldn't go—that he would stay, that he would choose her over everything else. But the other part, the part that had been pulling him toward Siachen for months, wouldn't let him. He couldn't make that promise. Not to her, not to himself.

So instead, he watched as she turned and walked away, her silhouette fading into the gathering twilight. The Chinar trees rustled in the wind, their leaves falling softly to the ground, and Arjun stood there, rooted in place, feeling as though something important had slipped through his fingers.

Saying Goodbye

The last few days before his departure were a whirlwind of preparation and goodbyes. Arjun packed his things, received briefings from his superiors, and made arrangements for the transition at the hospital. But in the quiet moments, when the bustle of the day had settled, his thoughts always returned to Zoya.

She hadn't spoken to him since that evening. They passed each other in the hallways, exchanged polite nods, but the warmth was gone. It was as though she had already begun the process of letting go, of preparing herself for his absence.

The night before he was set to leave, Arjun sat in the mess with Shashank, Raghav, and Mintu. The mood was subdued, and though they tried to keep the conversation light, he could tell they were all thinking the same thing.

"Here," Shashank said, sliding a shot of rum across the table to Arjun. "One last drink before you head off to the icebox."

Arjun chuckled, picking up the glass. "To Siachen," he said, raising it in a mock toast.

Shashank grunted, lifting his own glass. "To insanity," he corrected, smirking at him.

They clinked their glasses together, and the warmth of the rum burned its way down Arjun's throat, settling in his stomach. But it did little to chase away the cold that had been creeping in ever since he made the decision to volunteer.

The Morning of Departure

The morning of Arjun's departure came with an unsettling calm. The air was crisp, and the sky was a pale, icy blue as the sun rose slowly over the mountains. His bags were packed, his papers in order, and he was ready to leave.

But there was one last thing he needed to do.

He made his way to the hospital, his boots crunching on the gravel path as he walked. The familiar buildings loomed ahead, their whitewashed walls and red-tiled roofs glowing in the early morning light. As he approached the main entrance, he saw her.

Zoya stood there, her arms wrapped around herself, her face expressionless as she watched him approach.

He stopped a few feet away, unsure of what to say. The words he had rehearsed in his mind seemed inadequate now, hanging at the edge of his tongue but unable to form into anything meaningful. Zoya, in her usual grace and strength, stood there waiting, and for a moment he feared she had come to say goodbye for the last time.

"Zoya…" he began, his voice faltering.

She met his gaze, her eyes still filled with the lingering weight of everything unsaid between them. Her face was calm, but Arjun could see the emotion bubbling beneath the surface.

"You're going," she said, more of a statement than a question. Her voice was soft, controlled, but it carried the weight of a hundred unsaid goodbyes.

"I am," Arjun replied, taking a step closer, though the distance between them felt vast. "I wanted to see you before I left."

Zoya nodded, her eyes dropping to the ground for a moment before meeting his again. "I thought you might." She paused, taking a breath as if to steady herself. "I don't want you to leave without knowing something, Arjun. This past year… It meant everything to me. You meant everything to me."

The words hit Arjun harder than he expected. He had known, in the abstract, how much he meant to her, but hearing it like this, in the open air, with the mountains and the hospital looming behind them, made it real. Tangible.

"I meant everything to you?" he echoed, a faint smile trying to break through the tension in his chest. "And what about now?"

Zoya blinked, her eyes softening as she looked at him. "You still do, but I need to protect myself too. I can't hold on to you when you're going somewhere I might never reach. I can't stay tethered to a dream of us when you're choosing something else."

Arjun swallowed, feeling the words he wanted to say stick in his throat. The reality of the situation hung heavily between them, and the truth was, he had no rebuttal. She was right. By volunteering for Siachen, he was making a choice—a choice that wasn't about her, but about what he was willing to risk for duty, for his own sense of fulfilment. And he couldn't ask her to wait for a man who might not come back the same, or at all.

"Zoya, I wish I could make you promises," he said, his voice cracking slightly as he stepped closer. "But I can't. Not in this line of work. You deserve someone who can give you those guarantees, who can stay. I… I can't be that person right now."

Her eyes glistened, but she nodded, accepting what they both knew. "I know, Arjun. I knew from the beginning, but knowing doesn't make it easier."

She looked down, a tear slipping down her cheek, but she quickly wiped it away, her strength refusing to crumble. When she looked up again, there was a softness in her gaze—a mixture of love and resignation.

"I want you to come back, Arjun," she said, her voice barely above a whisper. "But if you don't, if this is it… I need you to know you mattered to me. That we mattered."

Arjun felt a lump in his throat as he nodded, reaching for her hand. She let him take it, her fingers warm in his, and for a moment, they stood there, connected by one last touch.

"You mattered to me too, Zoya," he said, his voice thick with emotion. "More than anything."

She smiled sadly, squeezing his hand one last time before gently pulling away.

"I'll be thinking of you," she said quietly, her eyes lingering on his for a moment longer. "Goodbye, Arjun."

And with that, she turned and walked away, leaving him standing there alone. The morning sun had fully risen now, casting long shadows on the ground as he watched her retreating figure, her steps measured and deliberate. Arjun wanted to call out to her, to stop her, to say something—anything—that could change what was happening between them. But he didn't. He couldn't. He had made his choice.

Where the Air Grows Thin

The journey to Siachen began in the afternoon. The flight to Leh was brief but breathtaking, the peaks of the Ladakh range stretching out beneath the plane like jagged teeth, each snow-capped summit gleaming in the crisp, clear air. From Leh, they would make the treacherous journey by road to the base camp at Siachen, the world's highest and most inhospitable battlefield. The thought filled Arjun with a strange mix of dread and excitement.

As the plane touched down in Leh, Arjun felt the familiar pull of duty surge within him, but the weight of his departure from Srinagar—and from Zoya—still sat heavily in his chest. The landscape here was stark and unforgiving, a barren wilderness of rock and ice that seemed to stretch on forever. There was no softness here, no warmth like the kind he'd grown used to in Srinagar. Everything about Leh felt like a prelude to something harsher.

Chapter 2

THE FROZEN FRONTIER

A Cold Welcome

The road to Siachen Base Camp was as treacherous as it was beautiful. Arjun sat crammed into the back of a Gypsy with his five new roommates, jolted around as the vehicle manoeuvred up the winding, snow-packed roads. The view outside was breathtaking—towering, jagged mountains capped in snow, their slopes vanishing into a white abyss below. But it was hard to focus on the beauty when the temperature was plummeting by the minute and the air was thinning so fast, each breath felt like a chore.

"Any of you think this is a bad idea?" Captain Rathod shouted over the rumble of the engine, his broad frame bouncing with every bump in the road. "Because I definitely think this is a bad idea."

Arjun chuckled, but the truth was, Rathod wasn't entirely wrong. Rathod, with his thick moustache and booming voice, was from Kolhapur, and it was clear he wasn't a fan of the cold. "Didn't you volunteer for this?" Arjun asked, grinning.

"I was pressured into it, Doc," Rathod said, adjusting his woollen cap, which looked like it was losing the battle against the biting cold. "Didn't think the glacier would be this cold! I should've stayed back in my place with the nice, warm sun."

Next to him, Lieutenant Banerjee snorted. Banerjee, slim and quiet, was from West Bengal, and despite his small frame, there was a steeliness about him that made you think twice before underestimating him. "You'll get used to it," Banerjee said dryly. "Or you'll freeze solid and become part of the glacier. Either way, you'll stop complaining."

Rathod let out a deep laugh, but before he could respond, the Gypsy hit another rough patch, sending them all lurching forward.

"This driver thinks we're goats!" Captain Ravinder Singh shouted from the front, gripping the dashboard with both hands. He was a tall man from Punjab, his turban tightly wound and his face hidden behind a thick beard that seemed tailor-made for the cold. "If we don't reach base camp soon, I'm going to lose more weight than I already have!"

Singh's comment made everyone laugh. He was known for his good-natured sense of humour, and in the freezing confines of the Gypsy, his light-heartedness was a welcome distraction.

After what felt like hours, the Gypsy finally slowed down, and the base camp came into view. The sprawling cluster of barracks and makeshift buildings looked like they had been carved out of the snow itself, nestled among the towering peaks of the Karakoram Range. This would be their home for the next two months—Siachen Base Camp—the last stop before soldiers were sent to posts scattered across the glacier.

The Gypsy came to a halt, and they all climbed out, greeted immediately by the sharp, biting wind. Despite the layers of clothing they wore, the cold was brutal, cutting through them as if they were standing in nothing but their skivvies. The altitude hit Arjun hard, and he found himself gasping for breath as he grabbed his duffel bag and looked around.

"Bloody hell," Rathod muttered, his breath visible in the freezing air. "It's colder than my ex-wife's heart out here."

Lieutenant Yadav, who had been mostly silent throughout the ride, raised an eyebrow. "You have an ex-wife?"

"No," Rathod said, grinning. "But if I did, she'd be as cold as this place."

They all laughed, but the sound quickly faded when they noticed Colonel Ramesh Rao, the commanding officer of the base camp, standing nearby with his arms crossed over his chest. He was a tall, lean man, his face deeply tanned weathered by his time in these harsh conditions. His sharp eyes scanned them as they approached.

"Welcome to Siachen Base Camp, gentlemen," he said in a voice that was somehow both stern and welcoming. "You're about to experience two of the most challenging months of your life. Up here, the glacier is your only enemy, and it's an enemy that shows no mercy. But if you survive the next eight weeks of training, you'll be ready for whatever the glacier throws at you."

He paused, letting his words sink in. "Get settled in. Your training starts at dawn."

The men exchanged glances—there was no time to waste.

Comrades in Quarters

Their barracks were simple, unheated, and functional. Six of them shared the space, crammed into a small room with cots lined against the walls. The only source of warmth came from a small, ancient heater in the corner that looked like it hadn't been replaced since the last ice age.

Arjun dropped his bag on the cot nearest to the heater and began unpacking, glancing around at his new roommates.

Captain Rathod was already complaining about the cold, despite wearing two extra layers of woollen sweaters. His big frame barely fit in his cot, and he fiddled with his woollen cap, muttering under his breath. "This heater better work, or I swear I'll freeze to death by morning."

"Stop crying, Rathod," Banerjee said, rolling his eyes as he methodically unpacked his belongings. "You're not in Kolhapur anymore. You volunteered for this. Man up."

"I did not volunteer!" Rathod protested. "I was misled! They told me it would be 'character-building'!"

Yadav, who was quietly arranging his own gear, smirked. "What character? Frozen solid?"

Lieutenant Singh, always ready with a joke, leaned over and pointed at Rathod's massive boots. "No, no. He'll thaw out once he gets moving. Rathod is a diesel engine—slow to start, but once he gets going, he'll be hard to stop."

Laughter echoed through the room, easing the tension of the cold and altitude. Humour, it seemed, was going to be the only thing keeping them sane here.

Arjun introduced himself properly, shaking hands with each of the men. "Captain Arjun, Army Medical Corps. I'll be the one patching you all up when this 'character-building' knocks you down."

Singh grinned. "Glad to have you on board, Doc. I've got a feeling we'll be needing your services soon."

"And me," Rathod added, still fiddling with his cap. "I might need a doctor if my ears freeze off."

"You'll be fine," Arjun said, smiling. "Just don't lose any limbs before training even starts."

The Training Begins

The next morning, as promised, Colonel Rao and their training officer, Major Mehta, had them up at the crack of dawn. The temperature had dropped even further overnight, and by the time they lined up outside with fifty other jawans for roll call, Arjun's fingers and toes were already numb, despite the thick gloves and boots he wore.

Major Mehta, a tough, no-nonsense officer with a perpetual frown on his face, stood in front of them, his voice sharp and clear. "Welcome to hell, gentlemen," he said without preamble. "Over the next eight weeks, we will push you to your limits, both physically and mentally. The glacier doesn't care if you're an officer or a jawan, if you're young or old, if you're from the plains or the mountains. The glacier treats everyone equally—and that means it will try to kill you equally."

Banerjee leaned over and whispered to Arjun, "I think he's trying to motivate us."

"I'm already motivated," Rathod muttered from the other side. "Motivated to stay in bed."

"Shut up, Rathod," Singh said, nudging him with his elbow. "Let the man speak."

Major Mehta continued. "Your first task today is acclimatisation. We'll be taking you up to a higher ridge, where you'll experience what it's like to walk in the higher altitude. You'll carry your packs, and you'll move as if your life depends on it—because one day, it might."

Arjun could feel the unease settling in among the group as they shouldered their heavy packs and began the ascent. The air was already thin, and as they climbed higher, it felt like breathing through a straw. His legs burned with each step, and his lungs struggled to draw in enough oxygen.

Behind him, Rathod was panting heavily, his breath coming in sharp gasps. "This… this is insane," he wheezed. "Who… who does this for fun?"

"You're doing great, Rathod!" Arjun called over his shoulder, trying to keep the mood light.

"I… hate you, Doc," Rathod gasped. "And I hate this place."

Banerjee, who was ahead of them, turned around and gave Rathod a rare smile. "You'll get used to it. Or you'll pass out, and then it won't matter."

Rathod shot him a glare, but his exhaustion was too great to respond. Singh, on the other hand, was laughing through his own heavy breaths. "Rathod, if you pass out, I'm not carrying you. I've got enough weight on my back already."

"Thanks, Singh," Rathod muttered, barely able to form the words. "Good to know I can count on you."

The banter helped, at least mentally. The physical challenge, however, was relentless. The higher they climbed, the more it felt like the cold and altitude were conspiring against them. Every muscle in Arjun's body screamed for rest, but they kept moving, driven not only by Major Mehta's orders but by the knowledge that giving up wasn't an option.

Finally, after what felt like hours of hiking, they reached the ridge. The view was staggering—an endless panorama of white snow and jagged peaks, stretching as far as the eye could see. It was a beauty that demanded silence, but all any of them could manage were gasps for breath as they dropped their packs and collapsed into the snow.

"Look at that," Banerjee said quietly, his eyes scanning the horizon. "It's… unreal."

Arjun nodded, too tired to speak. The sheer scale of the landscape was overwhelming, but more than that, it served as a reminder of where they were—and how small and vulnerable they were in this frozen wilderness.

Colonel Rao, who had accompanied them on the climb, walked among them as they rested, his eyes sharp as he assessed each man. "This is just the beginning," he said, his voice calm but authoritative. "Up here, your body will betray you. The altitude will make you weaker, the cold will steal your strength, and the isolation will test your mind. But you'll also find out what you're made of. By the end of this training, you'll either be ready for Siachen, or you'll know you aren't cut out for it."

Rathod groaned from the snow, his breath still labored. "I already know, sir. Can we head back now?"

Colonel Rao cracked a rare smile. "Not yet, Captain. We're just getting started."

The Gruelling Routine

As the days passed, the training grew tougher. Mornings started before dawn, when the temperature was at its lowest, and they spent every waking moment either hiking, climbing, or learning survival skills crucial to life on the glacier. Major Mehta seemed to take a perverse pleasure in pushing them to their limits, but it was clear to Arjun that his tough-love approach was exactly what they needed. There was no room for weakness here—every lesson was a potential lifesaver.

One particularly brutal day, they spent hours practising crevasse rescue drills. The glacier was filled with hidden dangers—deep crevasses that could swallow a man whole if he wasn't careful. Mehta had them practise how to anchor themselves into the ice, set up pulley systems to haul a man out, and work as a team in conditions where even a slight mistake could be deadly.

As Arjun was lowering Rathod down into a mock crevasse, Rathod looked up at him with a nervous grin. "Doc, if you drop me, I swear I'll haunt you."

"You weigh too much," Arjun grinned back. "If you fall, I'm going with you."

Singh, who was helping manage the ropes, chimed in. "If both of you go down, I'll pretend I didn't see anything. Can't lose too many calories pulling you back up."

Rathod groaned but held on as they completed the drill, the banter keeping the mood light despite the serious nature of the exercise. Colonel Rao watched them closely, offering occasional advice but mostly letting them learn by doing. It was clear to all of them that survival here would depend on their ability to work together and trust each other.

The Real Test: Avalanche Drills

One of the most harrowing parts of their training was preparing for avalanches, which were a constant threat on the glacier. The unpredictability of the snow, combined with the sheer force of an avalanche, meant survival was often a matter of quick thinking and luck.

One morning, they were told they'd be simulating an avalanche rescue. They were taken at a training site after a gruelling hike to the location, Major Mehta explained the drill.

"There will be three buried dummies somewhere in the snow. You have to find them, dig them out, and stabilise them in under twenty minutes. In a real avalanche, that's about how much time you'd have before it's too late."

"Great," Rathod muttered under his breath, "we get to dig in the world's biggest freezer."

Mehta's sharp eyes fell on him. "You'll be doing more than digging, Captain. And if you want to freeze, that can be arranged."

Singh elbowed Rathod in the ribs. "I think he has your number, Rathod."

Rathod rolled his eyes but got to work. As the drill started, the group spread out in teams, using avalanche beacons and probes to search for the buried dummies. The snow was deep and compact, making every movement a struggle. Arjun's hands were numb despite the thick gloves, and even breathing felt like an effort as they worked in the thin air.

Finally, after what felt like an eternity, they located the first dummy. Banerjee, Singh, and Arjun began digging frantically, throwing snow over their shoulders as they worked to free the buried figure. The seconds ticked by, and every movement felt heavier than the last, but they managed to dig it out in time.

"Got it!" Arjun shouted as they pulled the dummy free.

Across the training site, Rathod and Yadav were working on another dummy, and from the look on Rathod's face, he was struggling with the snow.

"This is impossible!" Rathod yelled, his breath coming in ragged gasps. "I'm not built for this."

Singh called out, grinning. "Think of it as shovelling snow for a warm beach vacation later. You'll thank us when you're sunbathing."

Rathod didn't reply, but his grumbling could be heard even from where Arjun stood.

By the end of the drill, they were exhausted, their bodies drained from the effort of digging in the heavy snow. Major Mehta gathered them together, his expression neutral.

"Not bad," he said, which, coming from Mehta, was high praise. "But not good enough. You need to move faster. In a real avalanche, every second counts. You either save your comrades, or you bury them. Remember that."

They nodded, too tired to speak. As they trudged back to the base camp, the weight of what they were learning hit Arjun. Every day, they were being prepared for the worst, and out here, the worst could come at any moment.

Losing a Comrade

As the weeks passed, they began to settle into a routine. The physical demands of the training were relentless, but their bodies slowly adjusted to the altitude and cold. However, not all of them were adapting as well as hoped.

Lieutenant Yadav had been complaining of leg pain for the past few days. At first, no one thought much of it—aches and pains were common in the harsh environment. But as the days went on, Yadav's discomfort grew worse, and it became clear something wasn't right.

During an ice-climbing exercise, Yadav finally collapsed. They were scaling a steep ridge when Arjun heard Rathod shout from below.

"Yadav's down!"

Arjun turned and saw Yadav slumped against the ice, his face pale and his breathing laboured. Instinct kicked in, and Arjun quickly descended to Yadav, checking his pulse and trying to get a response.

"Yadav!" Arjun called, shaking him gently. "Can you hear me?"

Yadav groaned softly, his eyes barely open. His breathing was shallow, and his legs, swollen and tender, pointed to the possibility of deep vein thrombosis (DVT)—a blood clot in his leg that had likely travelled to his lungs, causing a pulmonary embolism.

"We need to get him down, fast!" Arjun shouted to Singh and Rathod, who were already moving into action.

Together, they secured Yadav and began the arduous task of getting him down the ridge. Back at the camp, they worked quickly to stabilise him, but Arjun knew Yadav needed more advanced medical care than they could provide in these conditions.

Within minutes, a helicopter arrived to evacuate Yadav to a lower-altitude medical facility. As the chopper took off, the group watched in sombre silence. Losing Yadav, even temporarily, was a harsh reminder of how fragile life was on the glacier.

"That could've been any of us," Rathod said quietly that night as they sat around the heater.

Banerjee nodded, his expression grim. "Yadav's tough. He'll pull through. But we need to stay sharp. No one's invincible up here."

The Final Push

With Yadav gone, the team felt smaller, but they pressed on. The final weeks of training were the most gruelling yet. Each day was a new test of endurance, both mental and physical. The group, now seasoned by the brutality of their surroundings, knew the end of training was in sight, but they also knew the real challenge was still to come.

One of the last exercises was a multi-day trek to a higher observation post on the glacier. This trek simulated deployment to a forward post, where the men would have to manage not just the altitude and cold, but their own dwindling energy reserves and morale.

The first day of the trek was brutal. The climb was steep, the air thin, and each step felt like a battle against gravity. Rathod, unsurprisingly, had something to say about it.

"If I don't die from exhaustion," he muttered as they reached a particularly steep incline, "I'll die from boredom. How much longer, Doc? You got any medicine for misery?"

Arjun laughed between gasps for breath. "If I had medicine for this, Rathod, I'd be rich."

Banerjee, ever the quiet one, added, "If he dies, Singh, make sure you get his rations. No point wasting food."

Singh grinned. "Oh, I've been watching him closely. The second he drops, those extra chapatis are mine."

Rathod shook his head, smiling despite himself. "I'm not dying so you can eat better."

But despite the banter, the toll on all of them was evident. By the second day of the trek, the temperatures had plummeted even further, and the thin air made it feel as though there was an invisible hand pressing down on Arjun's chest, making it harder to breathe with each step. The snow was deep, and every time their boots sank into it, it felt like the glacier itself was trying to swallow them whole.

They pressed on, step by step, through the relentless cold. Colonel Rao, who had joined them for the trek, moved ahead of them with ease. He rarely spoke, but when he did, his words carried weight.

"This is what it's like out there," he said during one of their short breaks, gesturing to the endless stretch of white ahead. "Every day, this is what you'll be facing. The cold doesn't care about your comfort, and the altitude doesn't care if you can't breathe. You'll learn to survive, or the glacier will take you."

His words lingered in the air as they resumed their climb. It became clear that the real challenge wasn't just physical—it was mental. The glacier was indifferent to their suffering, and they had to find a way to push through that indifference.

A Moment of Crisis and Reaching the Observation Post

By the third day of the trek, they were nearing the observation post, a small, desolate outpost perched on a ridge overlooking the glacier. The weather had taken a turn for the worse, with heavy snowfall making visibility almost nonexistent. Exhaustion weighed heavily on all of them, but they pushed forward, knowing the post wasn't far off.

As they trudged through the blizzard, Rathod, who had been lagging behind, suddenly stumbled and collapsed into the snow. Banerjee, who was walking ahead of him, immediately turned back.

"Rathod!" Banerjee shouted over the wind. "Get up, man!"

But Rathod didn't move. Arjun rushed over, his heart pounding in his chest as he knelt beside Rathod, shaking him gently. His face was pale, his lips turning blue, and his breathing was shallow.

"He's hit his limit," Arjun muttered, checking his pulse. It was weak but steady. "We need to get him to the post, now."

Singh and Banerjee sprang into action, helping Arjun lift Rathod. The observation post was close, but the cold was relentless, and Rathod's condition was deteriorating quickly. His body was succumbing to the freezing temperatures, and his breathing was laboured—a clear sign of hypothermia setting in. They couldn't afford to waste any time.

With Rathod supported between them, they trudged through the snow, fighting the biting wind with every step. The post came into view like a distant promise of safety—a cluster of wooden structures half-buried in snow. The soldiers stationed there must have spotted them because as they approached, they rushed out to help, taking Rathod from their arms and guiding them inside.

The moment they entered, the warmth hit them like a wave. They placed Rathod near the fire, and the soldiers immediately began treating him for hypothermia. His lips were still blue, and his breathing remained shallow, but after wrapping him in blankets and carefully rubbing his hands and feet to restore circulation, he slowly started to stabilise. It was a close call, but they had made it in time.

When Rathod finally came to, he blinked up at them, groggy but alive. "You lot are the worst company," he mumbled, his voice weak. "I pass out, and no one offers me a chai?"

Singh grinned, patting Rathod on the shoulder. "We'll get you a chai now that we've reached the post. You're not getting out of this trek that easily."

Rathod smiled faintly, his spirit still intact despite the ordeal. "Glad to know you care."

As they gathered around the fire, sipping the hot tea offered by the soldiers, they finally began to thaw. The outpost was a modest collection of small wooden structures, manned by a handful of men who had been stationed there for months. Despite the brutal conditions, the soldiers greeted them with weary smiles, clearly accustomed to the isolation and the harshness of life on the glacier.

The soldiers shared stories of life at the post, and as they listened, it became clear that the glacier didn't just test your body—it tested your mind. The unrelenting cold, the isolation, and the knowledge that you were cut off from the world weighed heavily on even the toughest of men. But the soldiers had learned to cope through humor, camaraderie, and sheer willpower.

One of the soldiers, a grizzled old havaldar with a thick beard, leaned over to Rathod, who was still pale but recovering.

"Welcome to Siachen," the havaldar said with a grin. "You get used to the cold after a while. Or maybe you just go numb."

Rathod, never one to miss a beat, smirked. "I think I'm already numb. Can't feel my toes."

"You'll be fine," Arjun said, smiling.

The Final Weeks

After their trek to the observation post, the last few weeks of training passed in a blur of exhaustion and routine. The exercises continued to push them, but they were becoming stronger, more resilient. The altitude still made every breath a struggle, and the cold was as unforgiving as ever, but they had learned to adapt.

They spent hours practising everything from avalanche rescues to snow shelter construction, preparing for every possible scenario the glacier could throw at them. The physical challenges were brutal, but it was the psychological strain that took the biggest toll. By the end of each day, they were too tired to talk, collapsing onto their cots in the barracks, their bodies aching from the cold and the constant exertion.

But through it all, they had each other. The banter, the jokes, the shared misery—it kept them going. Even Rathod, despite his close call with hypothermia, never lost his sense of humour.

One night, as they sat around the heater in their barracks, Singh looked over at Rathod and grinned. "You know, Rathod, I've decided to write a book about this experience."

"Oh yeah?" Rathod said, raising an eyebrow. "What's it called?"

"'How to Freeze Your Ass Off in Ten Days,'" Singh replied, and the room erupted into laughter.

Even Banerjee cracked a smile, and for a moment, the cold seemed to disappear, replaced by the warmth of friendship and shared hardship.

The End of Training

The final day of training arrived with little fanfare. After weeks of gruelling physical and mental challenges, the men stood together in front of Colonel Rao and Major Mehta, who both looked at them with something approaching pride.

"You've all made it through," Major Mehta said, his voice sharp but sincere. "Most men wouldn't. But now, your real test begins. You'll be stationed at different posts across the glacier, and it'll be up to you to survive. The glacier has no mercy, but you've proven that you have what it takes to face it."

Colonel Rao stepped forward. "You've earned your place here. Take what you've learned and use it. And remember—out there, the only thing you can rely on is each other."

The men were given their assignments—Singh would be heading to a high-altitude post in the northern sector, Banerjee would be stationed in the southern sector overseeing communications, and Rathod would be stationed along with Arjun in the same company. Arjun was assigned to a medical support post attached to the company headquarters in the central glacier.

As they packed their gear for their final departures, a sense of both relief and apprehension filled the air. They had survived the brutal training, but now the real challenge awaited them. Each of them would be heading to a different part of the glacier, where the isolation and dangers would be magnified. The camaraderie they had built during the past two months would now be stretched across miles of frozen wilderness.

Rathod, despite his usual grumbling, was surprisingly quiet as he gathered his things.

"You nervous?" Arjun asked, strapping his pack onto his shoulders.

He shrugged, fiddling with his cap. "I mean, you get used to the cold, right?" he said, trying to sound casual. "But I won't lie. It was better when we were freezing together. Now I have to rely on myself."

Arjun grinned at him. "Trust me, you'll be fine. Besides, it's not like you're going far. We'll be in radio contact, and when you're bored, you can come down to my post for a visit. Maybe I'll even have some chai ready for you."

Rathod smirked. "You better. And you'll patch me up when my fingers fall off from the cold?"

"I'll keep the heater on for you. You'll be fine."

Captain Singh, who was heading to the highest post among them, appeared more excited than apprehensive. "I'm telling you, this high-altitude stuff is in my blood," he said, flexing his arms. "Punjabi mountain man, that's what I'm becoming."

"I thought you were a 'diesel engine,'" Banerjee teased, packing his gear with his usual precision.

Singh laughed. "I'm both. And when I come back, I'll have grown a beard so thick it'll make this cold run for cover."

"I'll believe it when I see it," Banerjee muttered, though there was a glint of amusement in his eyes.

The men turned to Banerjee, who was preparing to depart for his assignment as a communications officer in the southern sector. His quiet demeanour had kept him somewhat of a mystery, but over time, the group had come to respect his sharp intellect and steely resolve.

"Anything profound to say before you disappear into the snow, Banerjee?" Rathod asked, grinning as he adjusted his pack. "You're the philosopher of the group, after all."

Banerjee gave him a deadpan look. "Don't freeze. That's all the wisdom you're getting from me."

They all chuckled, but the laughter faded as the reality of their situation settled in. The next time they would see each other, if at all, could be months from now. And during that time, each of them would face the glacier alone.

Farewells at the Base Camp

The morning of their departure came swiftly. The Siachen Base Camp, which had become their home over the past two months, was now a place of farewells. Jawans and officers moved about the camp, preparing for their respective deployments. The air was thick with a sense of finality.

Colonel Rao gathered the men one last time for a final word before they left. He stood with his usual commanding presence, looking over them with his weathered, knowing eyes. Major Mehta was beside him, arms crossed, his face as stern as ever.

"You've been through the toughest training the Indian Army has to offer," Colonel Rao began, his voice clear and measured. "What you've learned here is not just how to survive. You've learned how to push past your limits, how to rely on your comrades, and most importantly, how to face this glacier with respect. Because if you don't, it'll take you."

The men stood at attention, letting the gravity of his words sink in.

"Out there," Colonel Rao continued, gesturing to the vast expanse of white beyond the camp, "Your survival will depend on your skills and your mental strength. But remember—no one survives the glacier alone. Look out for each other, even if you're miles apart."

Major Mehta gave a curt nod, signalling his approval. "And don't forget your training. The glacier shows no mercy, but neither should you. Every drill, every exercise we put you through was for a reason. Don't let it go to waste."

With that, Colonel Rao dismissed them with a simple, "Good luck. Stay alive."

As the group dispersed, Arjun looked around at the faces he had come to know so well. There was an unspoken bond between them now, forged through hardship and shared suffering. But there was also the quiet understanding that each of them would have to face the glacier on their own terms from now on.

Rathod, Singh, Banerjee—even though they were heading to different posts, they would carry the camaraderie and strength they had built together. The laughter and banter that had helped them through the toughest days might be absent in the silence of the glacier, but it would live on in their memories.

Singh slapped Arjun on the back, grinning. "And when this is all over, we'll meet again at base camp, have a proper meal, and talk about how we survived the coldest place on Earth."

Banerjee gave a rare smile, his usually stoic face softening. "We'll survive. But make sure you write that book, Singh. Someone's got to immortalise this madness."

Arjun nodded at each of them, feeling a mixture of pride, camaraderie, and sadness. It was the end of their journey together, but the beginning of a new chapter for all of them. The glacier awaited.

Chapter 3

INTO THE ICE

Leaving Base Camp

The day Arjun and his team left Siachen Base Camp for their forward posts was nothing like he had imagined. After weeks of grueling training, endless drills, and acclimatization exercises, Arjun thought he was ready for anything the glacier could throw at him. But as he stood there in the freezing darkness, his pack heavy on his back, the biting cold cutting through the multiple layers of gear, the sheer magnitude of what lay ahead finally hit him.

They had been up since 3 a.m., woken by the harsh, piercing cold. After a brief puja, a ritual they hoped would offer them some protection from the unforgiving conditions, they moved silently toward the convoy of vehicles that had been aligned in the predawn darkness. The air was crisp, and every breath turned into small clouds in front of their faces. The stillness of the early morning was broken only by the soft murmurs of the men and the crunch of snow beneath their boots.

The convoy was a mix of officers, jawans, and local porters—men from nearby villages who had made this trek countless times for logistical support. The porters, wrapped in their own layers of weathered wool, moved with the ease and confidence that only years of navigating this treacherous terrain could bring. They had an instinctive understanding of the glacier, having been to the posts for years, carrying supplies and guiding troops through the ever-shifting ice.

The vehicles would take them as far as the road allowed, after which they'd be on foot, pushing through the snow toward the forward posts. Arjun glanced at Rathod, who stood beside him, adjusting his gloves and pulling his hat down lower to block out the cold.

"Ready for this, Doc?" Rathod asked, his breath coming out in short bursts, adding to the swirling mist in the early morning air.

Arjun exhaled slowly. "I think we're all as ready as we'll ever be," he replied, though deep down, he wasn't sure any of them truly understood what lay ahead. They had trained for this, but standing there, in the shadow of the world's highest battlefield, the uncertainty gnawed at him. Training was one thing. This was something else entirely.

They piled into the waiting trucks, engines already rumbling as they prepared for the climb up to where the roads would end.

As the convoy set off, the mood was strangely quiet. The ride was rough, the steep, winding path leading them deeper into the glacier's heart, where the temperature seemed to drop with every metre gained in altitude. When the vehicles finally came to a halt, they disembarked, and the porters quickly took the lead, guiding them from here on foot.

The snow crunched beneath their boots as they trudged forward, the cold biting at their exposed skin despite the layers of wool and down they had wrapped themselves in. The wind was sharp and unrelenting, cutting through even the thickest of coats, making every step feel like a battle against the elements.

Arjun glanced over at the others in the group. Rathod was walking ahead of him, his usual boisterous personality muted by the cold. Lieutenant Verma moved in silence, his expression unreadable as always, while Lieutenant Iyer trudged along with a small, grim smile on his face, as if he was secretly enjoying the challenge. The porters, locals who had grown up in the harsh conditions of the mountains, moved with practised ease, their faces barely visible beneath thick scarves and hoods.

They hadn't been walking for more than an hour when the true scale of the glacier began to reveal itself. Endless expanses of white stretched out in all directions, broken only by the towering peaks looming overhead. The sky was a brilliant blue, but the sun provided little warmth. It reflected off the snow, making the landscape almost blinding, and the silence—save for the occasional whistle of the wind—was deafening.

"Feels like we've stepped into another world," Iyer muttered, his voice muffled by the layers of wool wrapped around his face.

Arjun nodded, though he wasn't sure if Iyer could see it through all the layers of clothing. "I've never seen anything like this," he admitted. "It's beautiful, but..." he trailed off, not wanting to voice the other thought that had crept into his mind. It was beautiful, yes—but it was also unforgiving.

"It'll get worse," Rathod chimed in, his voice a little louder than necessary, as if he were trying to dispel the silence. "This is nothing. Wait until we hit the higher altitudes. You'll feel like your lungs are trying to escape your chest."

Verma, ever the realist, added, "That's the least of your worries. The wind gets stronger, and if you lose your way out here, there's no coming back."

Arjun couldn't help but notice how the landscape seemed to shift with each step they took. The further they moved into the glacier, the more alien it felt—like they were walking on the surface of another planet. The snow was untouched, pristine, and blindingly white, and the mountains towered over them, casting long shadows across the ice. The wind picked up, howling through the narrow valleys, and it became harder to hear one another.

Introduction to the Glacier

As the day wore on, the brutality of the glacier's environment became more and more apparent. The wind, which had been a steady companion since they left base camp, grew fiercer, slicing through their gear and stinging any exposed skin. Arjun's face felt raw, the cold biting into his cheeks and nose despite the scarves wrapped tightly around them. The sun, though still shining brightly, provided no warmth. It only made the snow's glare more intense, forcing them to squint through the whiteness.

At one point, Iyer pulled his goggles down over his eyes and muttered, "I'm going to go blind from all this white. It's like staring into a flashlight for hours."

"You'll get used to it," one of the porters walking beside them said. He was a local, accustomed to the harsh conditions of the glacier. His face was weathered from years of navigating these mountains. "The glacier doesn't care how prepared you are. It'll grind you down until you either adapt or break."

Iyer grimaced but nodded. "Comforting thought."

They trudged onward, each step feeling heavier than the last. The altitude was beginning to take its toll on them, and even simple tasks like walking felt monumental. Every breath was a struggle, as if the air itself was refusing to cooperate. Arjun could hear the others breathing heavily, their gasps for air sounding louder in the silence of the glacier.

"Is it just me," Rathod panted, "or does it feel like we're walking through quicksand?"

"It's the altitude," Arjun said, trying to keep his voice steady despite his own labored breathing. "Your body's not getting enough oxygen. You have to take it slow."

"Slow?" Rathod groaned. "I'm already going slow! Any slower, and I'll be moving backward."

Verma shot him a look, his brow furrowed. "Save your breath, Rathod. You'll need it."

He was right. As they climbed higher, the air grew thinner, and more of them began to feel the effects of altitude sickness. Headaches, nausea, and dizziness hit each of them in waves. Arjun found himself stopping every few steps to catch his breath, and when he wasn't struggling with his own symptoms, he was helping others.

At one point, a young soldier stumbled and fell to his knees. His face was pale, and he clutched his head as if it were about to split open. Arjun rushed over to him, checking his pulse and asking a few basic questions to assess his condition.

"Headache?" Arjun asked, and the soldier nodded weakly.

"Feels like my brain is trying to escape through my skull," the soldier muttered.

"You're experiencing altitude sickness," Arjun explained, pulling out a small oxygen tank from his pack and fitting the mask over the soldier's face. "Take a few breaths of this, and you should start to feel better. But we need to keep an eye on you. If it gets worse, we'll have to get you back to lower ground."

As the soldier breathed in the oxygen, his colour began to improve, and after a few minutes, he was able to stand again. But the experience served as a reminder of how dangerous the glacier could be. They hadn't even reached the halfway point of their journey on the first day, and already, the environment was taking its toll.

Treacherous Terrain

The glacier wasn't just physically demanding—it was dangerous. As they moved higher, the terrain became more treacherous. They found themselves navigating narrow ridges, where one wrong step could send them tumbling down into the abyss below. The snow beneath their boots was packed tightly, but hidden ice patches made the footing precarious.

"Watch your step!" one of the porters called out as they approached a particularly narrow section of the trail. "The snow here is thin. One wrong move, and you're sliding all the way to the bottom."

Arjun glanced down at the crevasse below, its jagged edges barely visible through the snow. His stomach churned as he realised how far they'd fall if they lost their balance.

Rathod, walking ahead of him, muttered, "Why didn't I become a chef? Chefs don't fall into crevasses."

Verma, who had already crossed the narrow section and was waiting on the other side, called back, "Chefs also don't get paid to freeze on the highest battlefield in the world. Now hurry up."

They moved slowly, carefully, each of them taking turns crossing the ridge one by one. The wind picked up again as Arjun stepped onto the narrow path, and for a moment, he felt the ice beneath his boots shift. His heart pounded in his chest as he steadied himself, focusing on each step, making sure his footing was solid.

As he reached the other side, he exhaled a breath he hadn't realised he was holding. "That was… unnerving," he said, turning to Rathod, who was a few steps behind him.

"Unnerving?" Rathod scoffed, taking another careful step onto the narrow ridge. "That was outright terrifying. I thought I'd be a snowball rolling down into the crevasse.

Next time, remind me to stay at base camp and be a paper-pusher."

"Too late for that, my friend," Arjun said with a grin, though his own heart was still racing from the close call.

Once they were all safely across, the porters gave them a few moments to catch their breath before they continued on. The terrain was becoming increasingly unpredictable, with the glacier's jagged, icy surface constantly shifting underfoot. As they progressed, the snow deepened, and each step seemed to sink them deeper into the frozen ground, making it harder to lift their feet.

By the time they reached the icefall, an even more dangerous section of the glacier, the sun was beginning to sink lower in the sky. The icefall was a steep, frozen cascade where massive blocks of ice—some as tall as buildings—had formed over time, creating a labyrinth of towering ice walls and treacherous slopes.

The convoy came to a halt, and the lead porter motioned for them to gather around. His face looked as though it had been carved from the glacier itself—hard, weathered, and unyielding.

"Alright, listen up," he said, his voice gruff but clear. "We're about to cross the icefall. It's one of the most dangerous parts of the journey. Keep your eyes open and your feet steady. Watch for cracks in the ice—one wrong step, and you're looking at a long fall."

Arjun glanced at the massive ice walls ahead and felt a surge of unease. Crossing the icefall wasn't about physical strength—it was about mental focus. The slightest distraction could mean disaster.

"Why do I feel like I'm in one of those mountaineering documentaries where half the team falls into a crevasse?" Rathod muttered beside him.

"Because we practically are," Verma said dryly, tightening the straps on his pack. "Just don't be the guy who falls."

Iyer, always the optimist, gave Rathod a playful shove. "Don't worry, Rathod. If you fall, I'll come visit your memorial. I'll even bring flowers."

"Flowers won't help when I'm buried under fifty feet of ice," Rathod groaned. "Let's get this over with."

The crossing was slow and meticulous. They moved one by one, following the porters as they guided them through the maze of ice. Each step had to be calculated, each movement deliberate. The ice beneath them was unpredictable, sometimes solid and firm, other times cracking ominously underfoot.

At one point, the path narrowed, forcing them to cross over a small but deep frozen river that wound its way through the glacier. The ice on top was slick and smooth, and they had to move carefully, using ropes to secure themselves as they stepped across.

"Rope yourself in," the porter instructed as they reached the edge of the river. "The ice is thick enough, but it's slippery as hell. One slip, and you'll be sliding down the river before you know what hit you."

Arjun did as instructed, fastening the rope securely around his waist and following Iyer across the frozen surface. His boots slipped slightly on the smooth ice, but the rope held firm, giving him the confidence to keep moving.

As they reached the other side, Rathod let out a breath of relief. "I swear, the glacier's trying to kill us at every turn."

"That's because it is," Arjun replied, tightening the rope around his waist. "But we're not going to let it win."

Camaraderie in the Cold

Despite the dangers of the glacier—or perhaps because of them—a strong sense of camaraderie began to form among the men as the journey continued. Each night, after hours of navigating treacherous terrain and battling the relentless cold, they would set up camp, huddling together inside their tents to escape the freezing temperatures.

Inside those small, cramped tents, there was no room for pretence. The cold stripped away any need for formality or rank, and they found themselves talking freely—sharing stories, jokes, and the occasional complaint about the unforgiving environment. It was during these moments that Arjun began to see how essential this camaraderie was. Without it, the glacier's isolation could easily overwhelm a man's spirit.

One night, as they huddled around the heater in the tent, Rathod was rubbing his hands furiously, trying to get the feeling back in his fingers. "You know," he said, his voice muffled by his scarf, "I've been thinking, maybe we should write a survival manual. Call it 'How to Not Freeze to Death in Siachen.'"

Iyer chuckled, propping his boots near the heater, steam rising from the melting snow. "Step one: don't come here in the first place. I'll contribute that chapter."

Rathod grinned. "Step two: Make sure you bribe someone to bring real coffee. None of this instant nonsense."

Verma, sitting across from them, looked up from his book and smirked. "Step three: Learn to talk to the wind. It's the only thing that talks back out here."

Rathod nodded sagely. "Exactly. We'll include a special section on the different kinds of frostbite too. 'Fashionable Frostbite: Why Blue Fingers are the New Black.'"

Arjun couldn't help but laugh, shaking his head as the banter carried on. It was ridiculous, but in a way, it made everything feel lighter, more bearable. The cold, the isolation, the endless white—none of it felt as harsh when they could joke about it.

Later that night, as Arjun lay in his sleeping bag, the wind howling like some wild beast outside the tent, he found himself smiling. They weren't just surviving the glacier; they were finding a way to laugh at it. And somehow, that felt like a victory.

Encounter with the Elements

On the fourth day of their journey, the glacier reminded them just how unpredictable and dangerous it could be. The morning started off relatively calm, with the sun shining brightly overhead and the wind little more than a gentle breeze. But as they made their way further into the glacier, dark clouds began to roll in, and the temperature dropped even further.

By midday, the wind had picked up, blowing snow into their faces and making it difficult to see more than a few feet ahead. The group exchanged worried glances, and it wasn't long before one of the porters called for a halt.

"Storm's coming in fast," he said, his voice barely audible over the increasing roar of the wind. "We need to find shelter. Now."

They quickly gathered together, huddling close as the porters led them toward an abandoned supply bunker built into the side of a rocky outcrop. The entrance was half-buried in snow, but it offered some protection from the raging storm. Inside, the bunker was cramped and cold, but it was sturdy enough to shield them from the worst of the wind. They set up their tents within the bunker's walls, reinforcing them against the stone as best they could. The storm was moving faster than any of them had expected, and by the time they finished, the wind was howling, and the snow piled up against the entrance like a wall. It felt as if they were sealed off from the world, cocooned inside while the storm raged outside.

The storm trapped them for days. There was no visibility outside—a constant, swirling whiteout that made it impossible to tell where the sky ended and the ground began. The wind battered the tents, threatening to tear them apart, and the temperature dropped to levels that made every moment feel like a battle for survival.

Inside the tent, Rathod shivered, pulling his sleeping bag tighter around himself. "So much for the nice weather," he muttered.

Verma, who was sitting across from him, nodded grimly. "The glacier's always waiting for the right moment to strike. Storms like this are why so many men don't come back."

"Thanks for the pep talk, Verma," Iyer said sarcastically. "Really boosting morale here."

Arjun chuckled, though the seriousness of the situation wasn't lost on him. The storm was dangerous—not just because of the cold and the wind, but because it forced them into isolation. Stuck in the tents for days, with no way to move forward or back, they had nothing to do but wait.

As the storm raged on, Arjun found himself called upon to deal with the first cases of frostbite and hypothermia. Several of the soldiers had been exposed to the cold for too long before they found shelter, and the biting wind had done its damage. One young soldier, barely out of training, had developed severe frostbite on his fingers, his skin turning white and hard.

"Lie still," Arjun told him as he worked on the soldier's hands, trying to warm them with whatever heat he could provide. "We'll get you through this."

The soldier winced as Arjun applied warmth to his frozen fingers, his face pale from the cold. "I didn't think it would be this bad," the soldier whispered, his voice shaky. "I knew it would be cold, but... this..."

Arjun nodded, understanding his fear. The glacier had a way of making even the most prepared soldiers feel helpless. "It's tough," he said, his voice calm as he continued working. "But you're tougher. You'll get through this. We all will."

The words felt hollow, but Arjun knew it was important to keep morale up. In the end, all they had was their ability to endure—to push through whatever the glacier threw at them, one day at a time. The storm had trapped them, but their will to survive would carry them through.

The Waiting Game

The days blurred together as the storm raged on. Stuck in their tents, Arjun and the others waited in the freezing darkness, passing the time by rationing their food carefully and sharing stories in the cramped, musty space of their temporary shelter. The sound of the wind was relentless, howling outside like an angry beast, but inside, they huddled together, trying to stave off the biting cold.

Despite their efforts, the freezing temperatures seeped through everything—their tents, their clothing, even their bones. The small heaters they had weren't enough to fight the full force of the storm, and at times, it felt like they were trying to stay warm in a freezer.

Arjun could see the exhaustion and frustration building in the men around him. Rathod, usually full of humour, was quieter than usual, huddled in his sleeping bag and muttering under his breath. Iyer, who had been so upbeat when they first started, had grown more subdued as the days dragged on.

"I'm starting to forget what the sun looks like," Rathod said one evening, his voice muffled by his scarf as he lay in his sleeping bag. "I swear, this place is cursed."

Iyer chuckled weakly from across the tent. "We're living in an icebox, Rathod. What did you expect?"

Verma, sitting silently in the corner, looked up from his book. "I think the glacier likes messing with us. It'll let us think we're okay, then hit us with another storm just to remind us who's in charge."

Arjun smiled faintly, appreciating their attempt at lightening the mood. But he knew, deep down, that they were all struggling. The cold was relentless, but so was the mental strain. Being stuck inside, isolated from the outside world, made it hard to stay focused.

Still, they had no choice but to wait. The storm had trapped them, and moving in such conditions was out of the question. So, they held on, surviving one cold, monotonous day at a time.

Emerging from the Storm

After what felt like an eternity, the storm finally began to subside. The wind that had howled outside for days began to quiet down, and the constant swirling snow settled, leaving the landscape eerily still. Arjun and the others slowly emerged from their tents, blinking in the harsh white light of the snow-covered world around them.

The scene outside was unrecognisable—snow piled high in drifts, and the mountains and glacier had been transformed into an endless expanse of white. Though the storm had passed, the cold remained bitter, and the men were wary of what lay ahead.

"We need to move," the lead porter said, his voice hoarse from days of being inside. "The glacier's shifted. The paths will be different now, but we can't afford to stay any longer."

Arjun nodded. Supplies were running low, and they couldn't risk another storm catching them in the same spot.

They packed up camp quickly, shivering in the cold air as they prepared to continue their journey.

As they set off, the landscape felt even more treacherous than before. The fresh snow had covered any visible trails, and the path they had been following was now a maze of new ice formations and snowdrifts. The porters led the way, moving cautiously through the altered terrain, but the glacier was unpredictable. Every step felt like walking on unstable ground, and Arjun found himself constantly scanning the horizon for signs of danger.

The weight of the days spent waiting for the storm to pass had left them all tired and worn down, but there was no turning back. They had to reach the forward post. It was only a matter of time now.

The Final Stretch: The Wall of Ghosts

The sound of helicopter blades thumping through the thin, frozen air above felt like both a reminder of their isolation and a distant promise of salvation. The team looked up through the blinding white sky, straining to see the faint outlines of the two army choppers. Their rotors sliced through the cold air, the echo of their engines reverberating off the glacier. The choppers were headed toward the forward post, heavy with supplies. For a moment, a sense of envy crept in, perhaps even desperation. The thought of being inside those choppers—warm, flying effortlessly over the treacherous landscape below—was almost too tempting. The choppers would be at the post in minutes, while the team still had to face the most dangerous part of their journey.

"Think they'd notice if we waved them down for a lift?" Rathod muttered, his voice barely loud enough to be heard over the wind.

A faint smile tugged at one of the team members' lips, though the cold had tightened the muscles in his face. "They'd probably tell us to suck it up," he replied, not entirely joking.

The helicopters veered ahead, disappearing over the ridge that marked the border between them and their destination. Between them and the post, standing tall like a sentinel, was the infamous Wall of Ghosts. A 1000-foot vertical ice wall that had loomed in their minds for days as they trekked toward it, growing larger and more ominous with each passing hour. Now that they stood at its base, its presence felt like a heavy hand pressing against their chests.

The stories about the Wall were as old as the conflict itself. Every porter, every soldier who had been through Siachen for more than one tour, had heard about it. Some had faced it, others had seen comrades fall on it. The Wall was said to be merciless, indifferent to the skills and courage of those who dared to scale it. The porters called it "The Wall of Ghosts" not just because of its otherworldly appearance—gleaming, sheer ice, blue-white and reflective in a way that distorted reality—but because of how many lives it had claimed.

One of the porters, a hardened, wiry man with more mountain experience than the rest of them combined, stepped forward. He looked up at the Wall and nodded as if acknowledging an old adversary. He turned to the group, his voice low but steady.

"Many have died here," he said in a matter-of-fact tone. His eyes locked onto theirs, and they could see the weight of those words resting heavily on him. "This wall… it doesn't forgive mistakes. Once you're on it, every step matters. Don't rush. It will kill you if you let it."

They stared up at the ice wall. The sheer, vertical face looked impossible. It glistened in the cold light, with jagged edges, hidden crevices, and patches of snow covering sections of ice so smooth and steep they might as well have been polished glass. The wind swirled around them, whipping past the rock formations and gusting up from the glacier floor, making the entire place feel alive, like the glacier itself was a breathing, moving entity.

Rathod broke the silence with his usual grin, though it seemed a bit forced this time. "So… who's going first? I'd rather watch someone else's disaster before making my own."

Still, the tight feeling in his chest remained as Arjun checked his harness one last time. The porters had already begun setting ropes, their faces showing no sign of fear but rather a kind of resignation. They knew this climb, they had done it before, but that didn't mean they liked it. They moved in silence, their every motion deliberate, as if respecting the dead they believed lingered on the wall.

The base of the Wall of Ghosts was steeper than they had imagined. It rose before them like a frozen wave, crashing upwards and disappearing into the white sky above. The first hundred feet were dotted with jagged rock formations and ice ledges that could offer footholds, but beyond that, the climb became almost vertical, a smooth expanse of frozen death.

The wind picked up as they stood there, contemplating their ascent. They could feel the glacier's breath, cold and sharp, cutting through the layers of insulation as if they were nothing. Even with their experience, the climb ahead would test everything they had learned. Every handhold, every step would be a battle against both the ice and their own instincts.

As the porters finished securing the ropes, one of them turned and nodded to the group. It was time. One by one, they grabbed their ice axes, gripping them tightly. The familiar weight was comforting, but it also served as a stark reminder that their survival hung on these tools and their skill to wield them.

"Remember," the porter warned, his voice carrying over the wind, "no sudden moves. The ice is treacherous. One slip, and you'll go down, taking anyone roped to you with you."

They didn't need the reminder, but hearing it made the reality even more acute. They checked their gear one more time, tugging on the ropes, testing the feel of the ice axe in their hands, feeling the cold metal through their gloves. The tension in the group was palpable, the collective realisation of what lay ahead sinking in. The Wall was not just a climb; it was a test of endurance, a battle of will against nature itself.

The first soldier led the way, jamming his ice axe into the frozen wall and kicking his crampons into the ice. The sound of metal crunching against ice echoed in the frigid air. Step by step, he worked his way upward, focusing on each movement, each calculated strike. There was no room for error here—any misstep would send him crashing down into the abyss below.

Behind him, Rathod muttered under his breath as he followed. "If I survive this, I'm filing for permanent desk duty. I don't care what anyone says."

The soldier had to suppress a smile. Rathod's humour, though dark, was the kind of thing that kept them all going. The wind whipped around them, tugging at the ropes, as if the glacier itself wanted to pull them down.

They were only a quarter of the way up when the real challenge began. The ledges they had relied on to gain altitude had disappeared, leaving only a sheer, vertical wall of ice. The blue-white surface was so smooth that it reflected the light in strange ways, creating illusions of depth where none existed. Every step now demanded absolute concentration. The ice axe found holds, but they were shallow, and the crampons barely gripped the slick surface.

The porters had already climbed ahead, moving with a fluid grace born from years of experience in these unforgiving conditions. They moved higher, almost as if they were part of the glacier itself.

Suddenly, Iyer's voice broke through the focus. "Careful, the ice ahead looks unstable!"

A glance down revealed Iyer hesitating below, pointing to a section of the wall where cracks had begun to spider from a foothold. The warning was clear—one wrong move, and that section of the wall could give way.

The path adjusted, avoiding the cracked ice. The heart raced—not just from physical strain, but from the constant awareness that one misstep could be fatal. The Wall of Ghosts demanded precision, and the fear of becoming one of its casualties was very real.

As the climb continued, muscles screamed from the effort, the weight of the gear pulling down with every step. The higher they climbed, the harder it became to ignore the icy chill seeping into their bones. The top of the wall still seemed impossibly distant, lost in the white sky. Breathing became laborious, every exhale visible in the freezing air, the oxygen thin and cold in their lungs.

They paused halfway up the wall, clinging to the icy face like insects frozen in place. Rathod, directly below, looked up. His face was pale, but his determination unshaken. "I'll be honest, I've had better days."

Despite the tension in muscles, a chuckle escaped. "This one's going to be hard to top."

Verma, climbing further down the line, chimed in. "I think we've already peaked. Let's just not become part of the mountain, yeah?"

The banter kept them grounded, but the physical strain was starting to wear on them all. The Wall had a way of making time stretch. Every foot gained felt like a small victory, and every glance downward reminded them of how far they still had to fall.

As they neared the final stretch, the wind grew fiercer. It howled through the ice crevices, battering them from all sides. The cold was relentless now, cutting through their gear as if it were nothing at all. Every movement felt laboured, as though the glacier itself was sapping their strength with each passing second. Fingers had gone numb, and the only sensation in their hands was the faint pressure of gripping the ice axe. Only fifty more feet, but it felt like a mile.

The top of the Wall of Ghosts remained shrouded in mist, the wind blasting snow and ice crystals into their faces. The helicopters that had flown over hours ago were long gone, leaving only the silence and the sounds of strained breathing. One by one, they moved, slowly edging closer to the summit. Each few steps involved driving the axe into the wall, finding a foothold, and checking to ensure the others were still with them.

Rathod, usually the joker, was now focused entirely on surviving the monstrous climb. His face was pale, lips blue from the cold, but his eyes remained sharp and determined. The exhaustion was starting to set in. Verma, trailing behind, kept his head down, concentrating on every handhold.

"Almost there," Iyer's hoarse voice called from below, trying to reassure himself as much as anyone.

But the Wall was far from done with them.

As they reached the final stretch, the ice became more unpredictable. The deep blue shimmer of the surface belied its instability beneath. Large cracks and fractures spider-webbed out in every direction, some so thin they were invisible until weight was placed upon them. Every step now felt like treading on glass, waiting for it to shatter beneath them.

Then, a loud crack echoed through the air. Everyone froze. The ice axe remained embedded in the wall, but no one dared to move. Breath caught in throats as they scanned the wall, trying to pinpoint the source of the sound. Another sharp splintering noise echoed from below.

"Watch out!" Iyer yelled, alarm in his voice.

A large section of ice just below Rathod began to shift. The cracks spread quickly, splitting the wall. The seconds stretched into eternity. Rathod reacted immediately, driving his axe into the nearest solid hold.

But it wasn't fast enough.

The ice beneath him gave way with a deafening roar. A massive slab of ice broke free, plummeting down the wall. The rope attached to the harness went taut, and for a heart-stopping moment, it seemed like the ice would give way as well.

"Hold on!" came the shout, bracing against the pull of the line.

Rathod dangled just below, swinging slightly. His eyes were wide, but his grip on the rope remained firm. The collapsed section of the wall continued to crash down the glacier, a cascade of ice shards tumbling into the abyss below. The sound reverberated, underscoring how close they had come to disaster.

Their eyes met. Rathod gave a shaky smile—a grin that said, "Well, that was close."

"Maybe this wall doesn't like jokes after all," he muttered, breathless, as he swung back into position, pressing against the ice.

A breath was released, one that hadn't been realized as held. "Let's get off this thing before it decides to take all of us with it."

They resumed the climb, more cautious than before. Every step now fought against the wind, the cold, and their bodies that were begging for rest. The final few feet of the climb were agonising. Their energy reserves were nearly depleted, but the top was finally within reach.

One by one, they hauled themselves over the top of the Wall, collapsing onto the snow-covered plateau. Gasps for breath filled the air as bodies trembled with exhaustion. The wind howled, but here at the top, it felt like they had conquered something greater than just a physical challenge. They had beaten the Wall.

Rathod, pulling himself up beside them, gave a tired laugh, though it sounded more like a cough. "I'm definitely retiring after this. No more climbing ice walls for me. I'll put that in my resignation."

A smile was the only response, too tired for words, as they stared out over the glacier. The forward post was visible in the distance, a small cluster of buildings barely visible through the mist and snow. After days of trekking through harsh conditions, and surviving the Wall, the post seemed like the first sign of hope they had seen in a long time.

Iyer made his way over, shaking the snow off his gear. "That was… something else. I don't think I'll ever complain about base camp again."

Verma joined them, a mix of relief and exhaustion on his face. "If that wall doesn't kill you, nothing will."

They sat in silence for a few minutes, each lost in their own thoughts. The Wall of Ghosts had taken many before them, and it had tried to take them as well, but they had made it.

Arjun stood up, legs still shaky, but the exhaustion was already being replaced by a strange sense of triumph. The Wall of Ghosts had tested them, pushed them to their limits, but they had survived.

"Let's finish this," Iyer said, adjusting his pack. "The post is waiting."

They gathered themselves, checked their gear one last time, and began the final stretch of their journey. The wind still howled, and the snow still fell, but something had changed. They weren't just surviving anymore—they were pushing forward, determined to finish what they had started.

Arrival at Kullu Top

After what felt like an eternity trudging through the frozen wasteland, the team finally caught sight of their destination—a small, desolate outpost perched precariously on a high ridge overlooking the glacier. The structures were simple and utilitarian, almost swallowed by the layers of snow clinging to them. Despite their appearance, they were the only signs of life seen in days, and the relief that washed over Arjun was palpable.

The outpost, known simply as Kullu Top, was manned by a small detachment of soldiers who had already been stationed there for months. As they approached, a figure emerged from one of the snow-covered buildings, waving them over. He wore layers upon layers of cold-weather gear, with only his eyes visible through his scarf and goggles. As they drew closer, Arjun could make out the insignia of a Major on his shoulder.

"Welcome to Kullu Top!" he called out, his voice carrying over the wind. "I'm Major Satvinder Sharma, Company Commander here. You've made it in time for the warmest part of the day—only minus thirty now!"

His attempt at humour was met with tired chuckles from the convoy. Major Sharma's eyes gleamed with a mixture of relief and weariness.

"Let's get you inside," he continued, gesturing toward the nearest building. "You'll freeze your noses off if you stand out here much longer. The glacier has no sympathy for fresh meat."

The convoy followed him inside one of the small buildings that served as the command post. Arjun immediately felt the sharp contrast between the biting cold outside and the relative warmth within. The air inside was thick with the smell of stale coffee and damp wool, but it was a welcome change from the freezing wind that had battered them for days.

"Warm up, and I'll give you the full rundown of what to expect here," Major Sharma said as they dropped their packs and removed their outer layers. "You're about to become part of the most isolated unit in the world. You'll be calling this place home for the next three months, so I hope you like snow."

As they warmed up, a second figure approached—a man with a weary but welcoming expression. He was dressed in an officer uniform with a stethoscope around his neck, his hair tousled and his eyes bloodshot, as if he hadn't slept properly in days. He extended his hand to Arjun, recognizing him as the incoming medical officer.

"Captain Mishra," he introduced himself with a tired smile. "The doctor you're replacing. Believe me, you couldn't have arrived at a better time—I've been counting the days until my replacement shows up. I was beginning to think the glacier had swallowed you whole."

Arjun shook his hand, grateful for the warmth of his grip. "Captain Arjun, reporting for duty. I'm ready to take over whenever you're ready to brief me."

Mishra chuckled. They exchanged a look of mutual understanding. Mishra's tenure on the glacier was coming to an end, and though Arjun could see the weariness in his eyes, there was also a deep sense of satisfaction. This was a man who had done his duty in one of the harshest environments on Earth. And though he was ready to leave, a part of him would always remain on the glacier.

The Handover

Once they had warmed up and settled in, Major Sharma led the team through a quick orientation of the post, explaining the day-to-day operations, the security protocols, and the constant battle with the elements.

"As you've probably noticed, this place is hell frozen over," Major Sharma said, half-joking. "The weather can change in an instant, so you've got to be ready for anything. And don't be fooled by the clear skies—avalanches, frostbite, altitude sickness, you name it, we've got it. But we make do."

After the briefing, Captain Mishra pulled Arjun aside for the medical handover. They sat in the small medical room, a cramped space that served as the post's clinic, with just enough room for a stretcher, a few cabinets of supplies, and a portable heater that hummed weakly in the corner.

"Here's the reality of what you'll face," Mishra began, leaning back in his chair. "Most of the cases will be altitude sickness, frostbite, and the occasional injury from soldiers slipping on the ice or getting caught in minor avalanches. But the real challenge here is keeping the men mentally stable. The isolation can be brutal. You're not just their doctor—

you're their lifeline. Some days, all they need is someone to talk to. Other days, it's much worse."

Arjun listened carefully as Mishra went over the medical protocols and the limited supplies they had on hand. He pointed out the essentials: oxygen tanks for severe altitude sickness, antibiotics for infections, and, most importantly, the mental health treatments—basic counselling techniques and exercises to keep the men engaged.

"When the glacier wears you down—and it will—you've got to keep morale up," Mishra said. "Trust me, Doc, the biggest enemy out here isn't the cold. It's the isolation. That's what'll drive a man to the edge. You'll see soldiers who are physically fine, but mentally… they're hanging on by a thread."

As the conversation continued, Arjun could see the toll the last few months had taken on Mishra. He wasn't just handing over medical supplies—he was handing over the responsibility of keeping these soldiers alive, both in body and mind.

"You'll be alright," Mishra said finally, placing a hand on Arjun's shoulder. "You've been through the training. You know what to expect. Just remember, up here, it's about survival—yours, theirs, all of us. And the glacier doesn't care who you are or where you come from. It only respects those who fight to survive."

The Changing of the Guard

The day Mishra's departure finally arrived was bittersweet. He packed his things quickly, eager to leave the glacier behind, but before he left, he pulled Arjun aside one last time.

"Take care of them, Arjun," he said, his voice serious. "These men are counting on you. It's not easy, but you'll find your rhythm. And remember—don't let the glacier get to you. Stay sharp, and stay strong."

Arjun nodded, shaking Mishra's hand. "Safe journey, Mishra. You've earned it."

With that, Captain Mishra boarded the convoy heading back to base camp, leaving Arjun behind at Kullu Top to take up the mantle of the outpost's medical officer. As Arjun watched the convoy disappear into the distance, he felt the weight of responsibility settle on his shoulders.

Chapter 4

THE THIN LINE BETWEEN LIFE AND DEATH

Captain Arjun lay on his cot, trying to ignore the biting cold that had seeped through the layers of blankets. No matter how tightly he wrapped himself, the cold always found a way to creep in, as if the glacier itself had fingers reaching through the walls of their makeshift room. The kerosene heater in the corner sputtered weakly, hissing in protest every few minutes. The little heat it provided was more psychological than physical.

Across the room, Major Sharma sat at their shared desk, hunched over maps and reports. His body language was tense, his shoulders stiff, and his brow furrowed with the burden of command—responsibility for the men, the mission, and for every soul stationed at this frozen outpost.

"You're going to burn a hole in that map if you keep staring at it," Arjun remarked, shifting under his blankets in search of a position where his toes weren't freezing.

Sharma grunted without looking up. "If it helps me figure out how we're going to survive the next few months here, it's worth it."

Arjun chuckled softly. "You've been through this before, Major. Haven't you learned the glacier doesn't care what we plan? It'll do whatever it wants."

Sharma sat back, rubbing his eyes with his palms. "You're not wrong, Doc. But if we don't plan, this damn place will swallow us whole." He glanced over at Arjun.

"Besides, someone has to be prepared for when everything goes sideways."

Just as Arjun was about to respond, a deep, distant rumble interrupted him. It was faint at first, barely audible over the howling wind outside, but unmistakable—the sound of an avalanche.

Both men froze for a moment, listening. The rumble grew louder, deeper, and more menacing, echoing through the frozen peaks.

"Damn it," Sharma muttered under his breath, standing up from the desk. "Not now."

The sound grew louder by the second, a low growl vibrating through the ground beneath them. The walls of their room shuddered, and a few papers fluttered off the desk as the tremor passed through the outpost.

Arjun was already on his feet, pulling on his boots and grabbing his thick, fur-lined parka. "How close is it?"

Sharma didn't answer immediately. He threw open the door and stepped outside into the biting cold, scanning the horizon. The wind howled through the narrow gaps between the buildings, kicking up fine, powdery snow that swirled in the air like a miniature blizzard. The sky was a dull grey, with no clear indication of where the avalanche was coming from, but the rumbling was unmistakable now.

"It's close," Sharma finally said, his voice tight with urgency. "Too close."

The Avalanche Strikes

The entire outpost sprang into action as the rumble of the avalanche grew into a deafening roar. Soldiers scrambled from their quarters, pulling on whatever cold-weather gear they could grab as they rushed toward the small bunker built into the side of the mountain—a last-resort shelter designed to withstand the glacier's fury.

"Move! Move!" Sharma shouted, his voice barely audible over the rising wind and the growing roar of the avalanche. "Everyone to the bunker! Now!"

Arjun was right behind him, his breath coming in short, sharp gasps as he sprinted through the thick snow. His boots sank deep into the icy drifts, each step a battle against the glacier's frozen grip. Around him, the soldiers were running too, their faces pale with fear, their eyes wide as they glanced over their shoulders at the mountainside.

The sound of the avalanche was deafening now, a monstrous roar of snow and ice crashing down with unstoppable force. Arjun glanced back and saw it—an enormous wall of white, a tidal wave made of snow, rolling down toward them at terrifying speed.

It was a sight that made his stomach drop. No amount of training could prepare a person for the sheer terror of seeing an avalanche up close. The ground beneath his feet trembled, and he could feel the icy wind of the avalanche's approach biting at his exposed skin.

Sharma reached the bunker first, throwing open the reinforced metal door and waving the men inside. "Come on! Move it!"

Rathod, always the joker, was one of the last to make it to the bunker. As he ran, his arms pumping furiously, he shouted, "Don't worry! If I die, I want a statue in my honor! Life-sized, made out of snow!"

"Shut up and move your ass, Rathod!" Iyer yelled, pulling Rathod by the arm as they both dove into the bunker just as the avalanche hit.

The avalanche slammed into the ridge with a force that felt like the world itself was collapsing. The ground shook violently, throwing snow and ice into the air. Arjun barely made it inside before Sharma slammed the door shut behind him. For a moment, the sound was unbearable—a deafening roar of snow and ice crashing against the walls, as if the glacier itself was trying to bury them alive.

Inside the bunker, the men huddled together, panting and shivering, their faces pale with shock. The only light came from the dim, flickering bulbs on the ceiling, casting long shadows across the cramped space. No one spoke. The only sound was the distant rumble of the avalanche as it slowly passed, leaving a heavy silence in its wake.

"Well," Rathod said after a moment, his voice breaking the tension, "that was… exciting."

Sharma shot him a look. "Exciting? You nearly got buried under half a mountain."

Rathod grinned, his face still flushed with adrenaline. "Yeah, but I didn't. And that's what counts, right?"

Sharma sighed, shaking his head, though there was a hint of a smile on his lips. "You're a damn fool, Rathod."

"Hey, I try to keep things interesting," Rathod replied, still catching his breath. "I mean, what's life without a little adventure?"

Iyer, leaning against the wall, wiped the sweat from his brow. "Next time, try to have your adventure somewhere that doesn't involve all of us getting flattened."

Rathod grinned. "I'll keep that in mind."

Arjun, still trying to slow his racing heartbeat, leaned against the wall and looked around at the other soldiers. They were all in one piece, no injuries—just shaken. But he knew the real danger wasn't over yet. Avalanches often caused secondary collapses, and the glacier was still shifting. They weren't out of the woods yet.

Sharma checked his watch, frowning. "We'll stay in here for another half hour, to be safe. If there's any more movement up there, we're not going anywhere."

The soldiers nodded in silent agreement. The bunker, cramped as it was, felt like the safest place in the world right now.

The Aftermath

After what felt like an eternity, the rumble of the avalanche finally faded, leaving only the sound of the wind howling outside. Sharma gave the all-clear, and the soldiers cautiously opened the bunker door. The sight that greeted them was nothing short of surreal.

The landscape outside had been completely transformed. What had once been a relatively clear ridge was now buried under several feet of fresh snow. The outpost's buildings were half-buried, with only the roofs visible through the thick blanket of white. The path they had taken to the bunker was gone, replaced by smooth, undisturbed snow stretching out in every direction.

"Looks like we're going to be digging for a while," Arjun muttered, stepping out into the cold.

Sharma surveyed the damage, his expression grim but composed. "We'll clear it. Everyone grab shovels and start clearing the main path. We need access to the barracks and the supply hut first."

The men moved quickly, despite their exhaustion, grabbing shovels and starting the long, grueling process of digging out the outpost. The snow was dense and heavy, and with each shovel full, it became clearer how much work lay ahead of them.

Rathod, never one to pass up an opportunity for humor, groaned as he lifted his shovel. "You know, I always dreamed of spending my days digging in the snow. It's really living up to the hype."

Verma, who was digging nearby, shot him a look. "If you spent less time talking and more time digging, we'd be done by now."

Rathod grinned. "Where's the fun in that?"

Despite the back-breaking labor, the soldiers worked together, their camaraderie evident in the way they joked and teased each other..

A Test of Endurance

Hours passed, and the soldiers finally began to make headway. The paths were cleared, and the barracks and supply huts were accessible again, but the work wasn't over. The avalanche had shifted more than just the snow—it had altered the landscape, making navigation difficult. There was an unspoken understanding among the men that the glacier could shift again at any moment, and there was an unspoken tension that kept them all vigilant. They had survived this avalanche, but no one was under the illusion that the danger had passed.

As they worked, Rathod continued to keep the mood light with his constant banter. "You know, if I wanted to spend my life shoveling snow, I could've taken a job at a ski resort. At least they have hot tubs and après-ski."

Iyer, who was digging nearby, wiped sweat from his brow despite the cold and shot back, "And those people don't have to worry about getting buried alive by a mountain."

Rathod grinned and lifted another shovel full of snow. "Details, details. You always focus on the negatives."

Arjun, listening to their exchange as he worked, couldn't help but smile. Rathod's humor was infectious. Every joke was a way to mask the fatigue, the growing despair that gnawed at all of them. Humor kept them going, but it didn't hide the fact that their situation was dire.

After hours of grueling work, the soldiers finally took a break. They gathered in the mess hall to rest their aching muscles and thaw out by the stove. The small wood burner struggled to heat the room, but it was better than being outside in the biting wind.

Sharma entered last, shaking the snow off his coat and pulling off his gloves. His face was red from the cold, and his hair damp from the exertion. He looked around at his men, who were slumped in chairs, their faces drawn with exhaustion.

"Good work today, everyone," he said, clapping his hands together for warmth. "We've made good progress, but there's still a lot to clear. Get some rest, and we'll head back out after a short break."

Rathod, sprawled out on a bench, groaned dramatically. "Short break? I was hoping for a week off, Major."

Iyer snorted from across the room. "In your dreams, Rathod. You'll be lucky to get more than thirty minutes."

Rathod sighed theatrically. "Thirty minutes? Major, you're killing my napping dreams."

Sharma, who had initially been in a grim mood, allowed himself a smile. "You can dream about naps after you've finished clearing the snow."

Rathod's head lolled back as he dramatically faked exhaustion. "I'll be the first man in history to die of shovel-induced fatigue."

Iyer, who was nursing a cup of kadha chai, chuckled. "You'd find a way to make even that sound like an achievement."

The soldiers laughed, their spirits temporarily lifted by Rathod's antics. For a brief moment, the grim reality of their situation faded into the background as they enjoyed the camaraderie that bound them together.

Conversation: Arjun and Sharma

The tent was dimly lit, the cold outside an ever-present reminder of the glacier's unforgiving nature. Arjun sat on his cot, gazing at the ceiling, his thoughts churning.

He turned his head toward Sharma, who was hunched over his logbook, scribbling intently. "Sir, can I ask you something?"

Sharma didn't look up. "If it's about rations or the radio again, Doc, the answers are no and still no."

Arjun chuckled lightly. "Not that. I was just wondering... why did you join the army?"

That made Sharma pause. He set down his pen and leaned back in his chair, stretching his arms. "Why does anyone join? Duty, honor, adventure... pick your cliché."

Arjun gave him a skeptical look. "You're not one for clichés. The real reason, Major."

Sharma sighed and leaned forward, resting his elbows on the desk. "Fine. If you must know, I joined because it was the only thing that made sense at the time. My father was in the army. Grew up listening to his stories of battles and camaraderie. Seemed like the logical thing to do."

Arjun nodded, sensing there was more. "And now? Does it still make sense?"

Sharma was quiet for a moment, his gaze fixed on the heater's flame. "Some days, yes. Other days... not so much. The weight of it all, the things we see, the decisions we make—it stays with you, you know? But leaving? That feels impossible too."

Arjun sat up straighter. "Sounds like you're carrying a lot more than just duty."

Sharma chuckled dryly. "You get good at it after a while. Or at least you pretend you are."

The silence between them stretched, heavy but not uncomfortable. Finally, Arjun broke it. "Do you ever regret it?"

Sharma looked at him, his eyes shadowed but sincere. "Regret? No. But there are days I wonder who I might have been if I'd chosen differently. Someone softer, maybe. Someone who didn't have to learn to bury things deep."

Arjun smiled faintly. "Well, for what it's worth, you're the kind of person I'd want watching my back up here."

Sharma's lips quirked in a small, tired smile. "Thanks, Doc. That means something. Especially here, where everything feels like it's trying to break us."

Arjun nodded. "It doesn't have to. We're still human. We can still talk, lean on each other."

Sharma stood, stretching out his stiff limbs. "You're an optimist, Doc. Don't let this place take that from you."

"And you're a realist," Arjun replied. "But even realists can afford to hope sometimes."

Sharma gave him a long look, then clapped him lightly on the shoulder as he headed to his bed. "Get some sleep, Arjun. Tomorrow, the glacier wins round whatever. But tonight, maybe we take a small victory."

Arjun watched as Sharma settled into his cot, the weight between them a little lighter, if only for the night

Coping with the Glacier

The days continued to blend together. The routine became mind-numbing—digging snow, checking equipment, rationing supplies. The physical labor was grueling, but it was the mental strain that concerned Arjun the most.

He saw it in the men's faces—their eyes hollow, their conversations sparse, and their movements slow. The isolation, the unending cold, the sameness of every day—it was wearing them all down.

Rathod, who had been the glue holding the group together with his jokes and antics, was beginning to fray at the edges. His humor had become less frequent, and there were moments when he would sit in silence, staring off into the snow as if lost in thought.

One evening, as the men gathered in the mess hall after another long day of digging, Arjun noticed that Rathod wasn't his usual self. The others were talking quietly, sharing stories from back home, but Rathod sat by the stove, staring into his cup of tea.

"You alright, Rathod?" Arjun asked, sitting down beside him.

Rathod looked up, blinking as if pulled from a distant thought. "Yeah, I'm fine. Just… tired, I guess."

"Tired?" Iyer chimed in from across the table. "That's a first—Rathod, tired of talking? Someone write this down."

The men chuckled, but Rathod didn't join in. He gave a weak smile and took another sip of his tea.

Arjun frowned. "You sure? You've been quiet lately."

Rathod shrugged. "Just feeling the weight of it all, Doc. This place… it's hard to keep joking about it when you wake up to the same freezing nightmare every day."

The room fell silent. Everyone understood what Rathod meant. No matter how much they laughed or how hard they worked, the glacier was always there—a constant, looming presence, as indifferent as it was unforgiving.

"We're all feeling it," Iyer said quietly. "But that's why we stick together. We get through it as a team."

Verma, always the optimist, nodded. "Yeah, Rathod. Don't go soft on us now. We need someone to make jokes about losing toes to frostbite."

That brought a smile to Rathod's face, though it was weak. He shook his head and took another sip of tea. "Don't worry, Verma. I'm not going anywhere. Just having one of those days, you know?"

Arjun placed a hand on Rathod's shoulder. "We all have those days. But if it starts feeling like more than a day, talk to me. We're in this together."

Rathod nodded, his eyes downcast. "Thanks, Doc. I'll keep that in mind."

Arjun spent most of his time checking on the soldiers, both physically and mentally. It wasn't frostbite and altitude sickness that concerned him—it was the slow unraveling of their spirits. The men who had arrived with laughter and energy were now hollow, their eyes vacant, their hands shaking as they performed their daily tasks. The cold didn't just freeze their bodies—it froze their minds.

One night, after another long day of digging and repairing equipment, Arjun sat on his cot, rubbing his tired eyes.

."Rathod's not looking too good," Arjun said quietly, breaking the silence.

Sharma didn't look up from his logbook. "None of us are."

Arjun sighed, leaning back against the wall. "I'm worried about him. He's always been the one keeping everyone's spirits up, but now… it's like he's slipping."

Sharma paused, set his pen down, and turned to face Arjun. His face was worn, and his eyes reflected exhaustion that went deeper than just a lack of sleep. "We're all slipping, Doc. This place—it wears you down, little by little. Even Rathod's humor can't hold out forever."

Arjun nodded slowly. "I just don't want to lose anyone. Not to this."

Sharma's jaw tightened. "We won't," he said firmly. "Not if we keep an eye on each other."

Arjun glanced at him, surprised by the sudden conviction in Sharma's voice. "You sound sure of that."

Sharma gave a grim smile. "I've seen worse, Doc. This place may be hell, but we've got each other. That's how we'll get through it."

There was a pause as Arjun absorbed his words. It was true—without the camaraderie, without the bond between the men, Kullu Top would be unbearable. The isolation, the cold, the constant danger—they were all things that could be survived if they stuck together.

"You're right," Arjun finally said. "But I'm still keeping an eye on Rathod. If he needs more than just a talk, I'll take action."

Sharma nodded. "Do what you need to. Just make sure we don't lose him. He's been the glue holding a lot of these guys together."

Arjun's role as the medical officer was increasingly becoming more about counseling the men than treating physical injuries. He found himself sitting with them in the mess hall or during the rare quiet moments in the barracks, listening to them talk about the weight of their isolation.

One night, a young soldier sat on his bunk, staring at his hands as if they didn't belong to him. Arjun noticed the tension in the man's shoulders, the way his fingers trembled slightly. He approached quietly, sitting down beside him.

"You alright?" Arjun asked.

The soldier blinked, not meeting his eyes. "I don't know, Doc. Everything's… every day feels the same. I wake up, I work, I sleep. The cold never goes away. It's like… it's inside my head now."

The soldier looked up at him, his eyes tired and hollow. "I don't know how much longer I can take it."

Arjun nodded, his expression soft but resolute. "One day at a time. That's how we get through this. And if it gets too much, come talk to me. You don't have to handle it alone."

The soldier gave a small nod, though the uncertainty remained in his eyes. Arjun recognized that look—he had seen it before in men who were reaching their breaking point. He knew he'd need to keep a closer eye on all of them, especially Rathod.

One evening, after several days of quiet tension, Rathod seemed to snap out of his funk. He walked into the mess hall with a grin on his face, and the mischief that had been missing for weeks was back in his eyes.

"Gentlemen," Rathod announced, jumping onto one of the tables, arms outstretched dramatically. "I have a proposition."

The men, slumped around the room, glanced up with mild curiosity.

"Since we're stuck here, freezing our asses off in the middle of nowhere, I propose we have ourselves a little celebration," Rathod said, his grin widening.

"A celebration?" Banerjee asked, raising an eyebrow. "What exactly are we celebrating?"

"Exactly!" Rathod replied, his voice full of mock enthusiasm. "We've been here for what feels like forever, and guess what? We're still alive! That, my friends, is worth celebrating."

Iyer, sipping from a mug of tea, snorted. "What are you suggesting, Rathod? A snowball fight?"

Rathod jumped down from the table, rubbing his hands together. "Close, but no. I propose the 'Kullu Top Olympics'—a series of challenges to test our survival skills, strength, and yes, our stupidity."

The men stared at him for a moment, then began to laugh, the sound of their voices echoing off the mess hall walls. For the first time in weeks, the oppressive silence was broken, and there was a sense of anticipation in the air.

Sharma, leaning back in his chair, looked at Rathod with an amused expression. "Alright, I'll bite. What challenges are we talking about?"

Rathod's grin turned devilish. "Oh, you'll see, Sir. By the time we're done, you'll be wishing for an avalanche to save you from the embarrassment."

The Kullu Top Olympics

The next morning, the soldiers gathered outside in the snow, bundled up against the biting wind but clearly excited about Rathod's proposed "Olympics." The day promised a brief escape from the monotony, a chance to laugh and push themselves in ways they hadn't done in weeks.

The first challenge was the Frozen Boot Toss, where each soldier had to hurl a frozen, ice-covered boot as far as they could across the snow. The second event was the Snow-Crawl Relay, a race that involved crawling through makeshift snowdrifts while trying not to collapse from laughter or exhaustion. The final event was the Ice Block Luge, where soldiers slid down a small hill on blocks of ice, attempting to make it to the bottom without wiping out spectacularly.

Sharma, who had been skeptical at first, found himself laughing alongside the rest of the men as they watched Rathod and Iyer tumble through the snow in the Snow-Crawl Relay. At one point, the relay turned into an impromptu snowball fight, with the men pelting each other and diving behind snowdrifts for cover.

"I have to admit, this was a good idea," Sharma said to Arjun as they watched the chaos unfold.

Arjun, grinning, nodded. "Yeah, I hate to say it, but Rathod's got a gift. This might not be in the manual, but it's keeping us all from losing it."

Sharma chuckled as Rathod attempted the Ice Block Luge and ended up face-first in a snowbank at the bottom of the hill. The soldiers erupted in laughter, and for the first time in weeks, the mood was light.

When the events wrapped up, Rathod, now drenched in snow and grinning like a madman, climbed onto a snow mound and raised his arms in triumph.

"I declare myself the Supreme Champion of the Glacier!" he shouted, his voice booming over the howling wind. "And as my first act as ruler, I hereby decree all soldiers are entitled to an extra ration of chai!"

The men roared in mock approval, clapping and cheering as Rathod puffed out his chest like a victorious gladiator. Sharma rolled his eyes but couldn't hide the smile tugging at his lips.

"I think Rathod's earned himself latrine duty for a month," Sharma muttered to Arjun, who laughed.

"Let him have his moment," Arjun replied. "He's keeping everyone going, even if it's through sheer stupidity."

A Glimmer of Normalcy

For the next few days, the mood at Kullu Top was noticeably brighter. Rathod's antics and the makeshift Olympics had worked wonders on morale, giving the soldiers something to smile about in the midst of their frozen reality. Even Major Sharma, normally so serious, seemed to have relaxed a little, occasionally engaging in light-hearted conversation during meals.

But as was the nature of life on the glacier, the relief was temporary. Soon, the weather shifted again, and a brutal snowstorm rolled in, bringing with it a sense of dread that hung over the outpost.

The men were confined to the mess hall as the storm raged outside, the wind howling like a wild animal. Visibility dropped to nearly zero, and the temperature plummeted, making the already difficult conditions unbearable.

Arjun stood by the window, watching the storm batter the outpost, the snow so thick it looked like a solid wall of white outside. He could barely make out the shapes of the barracks just a few meters away. Everything was swallowed by the storm.

Sharma joined him by the window, crossing his arms and staring out into the swirling snow. "It's always like this, isn't it? One minute, you think you're catching a break, and the next, the glacier reminds you who's really in charge."

Arjun nodded, his breath fogging up the cold glass. "Yeah, it never gives us too long to relax. The storm will pass, though. It always does."

Sharma didn't reply, but his eyes stayed fixed on the blizzard outside. Both men knew the truth—the storm would pass, but the challenges wouldn't. The glacier had a way of keeping its grip tight, always ready to remind them of how little control they truly had. Out here, nothing was permanent except the cold, the isolation, and the weight of their own thoughts.

The following day, after the storm had passed, Arjun and Sharma stood outside, surveying the post. The sun had broken through the clouds, casting a harsh, cold light on the snow-covered buildings. The wind had died down, leaving a strange stillness in the air.

"You were right," Arjun said, breaking the silence.

Sharma, his arms crossed and his eyes scanning the horizon, turned to him. "About what?"

Arjun took a deep breath, the cold air burning his lungs. "That we'd make it through. One day at a time."

Sharma gave a tired smile, his eyes softened with a rare hint of relief. "We always do, Doc. We always do."

They stood there for a few more moments, the silence stretching between them as they watched the men begin their daily routine—clearing snow, maintaining equipment, preparing for another long, cold day.

Chapter 5

THE SILENT BATTLE

The howling wind tore through Kullu Top as Captain Arjun stood, his eyes fixed on the edge of the ice wall. The sheer drop below loomed like an abyss, with the glacier stretching endlessly beneath, obscured by thick, swirling snow. The storm had not let up, and the wind's sharp bite made every breath painful, but none of that mattered now. All Arjun could think of was Naik Raghav, lying inside the infirmary, unconscious and fading fast.

Raghav had been hanging on for hours, but his condition was worsening rapidly. Cerebral Venous Thrombosis (CVT) had struck, brought on by the altitude and extreme cold, and the blood clot in his brain was stealing the life from him minute by minute. Time was running out, and the helicopter they had called for couldn't make it to their remote post, perched precariously on the ice wall.

Arjun's heart raced as he made his way back to the infirmary, where Raghav lay motionless, his breath shallow and labored. He glanced at his watch—every second felt like a countdown, a reminder that they were fighting a battle they could not afford to lose.

"Major Sharma," Arjun called, his voice tight with urgency as he found the commanding officer. "We need to get him down the ice wall now. The helicopter can't land here."

Sharma's face was grim, his breath fogging in the freezing air. "I know, Doc. But the descent..." He didn't finish the sentence, but the meaning was clear. The ice wall was treacherous on the best of days, and in the middle of a storm like this, it would be deadly.

"We don't have a choice," Arjun said, glancing at the door of the infirmary where Raghav lay. "If we don't move him, he's going to die here."

Sharma nodded slowly, then gave the order. "Get the stretcher ready. We'll need to move quickly."

Preparing for the Descent

Rathod and Iyer were already at the infirmary, their faces pale but determined. They knew the dangers of the descent as well as Arjun did. The ice wall was steep, slick with frost and snow, and one misstep could send them all tumbling to their deaths. But they also knew that staying put meant certain death for Raghav.

The stretcher was prepped quickly, and Arjun made sure Raghav was strapped in tightly. He bundled him in as many layers as possible, though he knew it wouldn't be enough to keep the cold at bay. The wind outside howled like a beast, and the temperature was dropping fast.

Arjun bent down to check Raghav's pulse again. It was faint, his heartbeat slow and erratic. His breath fogged in the air, coming in shallow gasps. Arjun's chest tightened with fear—he could feel time slipping away, and they needed to move now.

"Stay with me, Raghav," Arjun muttered under his breath as he stood up. He adjusted his own layers, tightening his gloves and scarf. The wind clawed at him the moment he stepped outside, and it was like walking into a wall of ice. His breath came in short bursts, and his vision blurred as the snow whipped around him.

The soldiers took up their positions on either side of the stretcher. Rathod and Iyer gripped the handles tightly, their boots digging into the ground as they prepared to move. Arjun stayed close to Raghav's side, his medical bag slung over his shoulder, his mind racing through every possible scenario.

"We'll take it slow," Arjun said, shouting over the wind. "One step at a time."

Sharma gave a nod from his position near the edge. "Ready?"

Arjun glanced down the ice wall—it was barely visible through the snowstorm. The path was narrow, with sharp drops on either side, and the ice shimmered in the dim light, treacherous and unforgiving.

"Let's go," Arjun said, his heart pounding.

The Descent

The first steps over the edge of the ice wall were slow and careful, each soldier moving deliberately, their boots crunching against the frozen surface. The storm lashed at them, and the wind threatened to pull the stretcher from their grasp with every gust. The cold bit into their skin, even through the layers of wool and fur, and Arjun felt his fingers numbing as he gripped the side of the stretcher.

The path was a steep incline, barely wide enough for the soldiers to walk side by side. The ice underfoot was slick, covered in a thin layer of snow that made every step a gamble. Rathod led the way, his movements slow but steady as he felt for solid footing. Behind him, Iyer kept his head down, his face grim with concentration.

"Easy now," Arjun called over the wind, his voice strained. "Watch your footing."

The stretcher swayed dangerously as they moved, and Arjun kept one hand on Raghav's shoulder, trying to keep him steady. He glanced down at the soldier's face—Raghav's skin was turning gray, his breath coming in short, shallow gasps. His pulse was weakening, and Arjun's stomach churned with dread.

They were halfway down the ice wall when disaster nearly struck. Iyer's boot slipped on a patch of ice, and for a heart-stopping moment, he lost his balance. The stretcher lurched to one side, nearly tipping over the edge of the narrow path. Rathod shouted in alarm, his grip tightening as he tried to pull the stretcher back.

"Hold it!" Arjun yelled, his heart hammering in his chest. He lunged forward, grabbing the side of the stretcher and pulling it back to safety. His legs shook from the sudden movement, and his breath came in ragged gasps.

Iyer managed to regain his footing, his face pale with shock. "I'm okay," he muttered, though his voice was shaky.

Arjun nodded, though his own nerves were frayed. "Let's keep moving," he said, though his voice was tight with tension. "Slow and steady."

They continued down the ice wall, each step more difficult than the last. The storm showed no signs of letting up, and the wind was relentless, tearing at them with icy claws. Arjun's fingers had gone numb, and he could barely feel his feet in his boots. The cold was seeping into his bones, and he knew it was only a matter of time before frostbite became a serious threat.

But they couldn't stop. Raghav's life hung in the balance, and every second they spent on the ice wall was a second closer to losing him.

By the time they reached the base of the ice wall, Arjun could hardly feel his fingers. His breath came in ragged gasps, and his legs trembled from the strain of the descent. The narrow path had widened slightly as they neared the bottom, but the ice was still treacherous, and the wind still howled around them like a living thing.

"Almost there," Rathod called over his shoulder, his voice hoarse from the cold.

Arjun glanced down at Raghav—his face was pale and slack, his breathing shallow. Arjun knelt beside him for a moment, checking his pulse. It was weak, barely there. His skin had taken on a bluish tint, and the frostbite was spreading across his fingers and toes.

"He's not going to last much longer," Arjun muttered under his breath, though the words felt like a punch to the gut.

They moved faster now, their desperation growing with each step. The snow crunched beneath their boots, and the path began to even out as they reached the base of the ice wall. In the distance, through the swirling snow, they could see the outline of the lower post, a small building that offered a brief respite from the storm. But it was still a long way off, and Raghav was slipping further with every minute.

On the Snow Scooter

Once they reached the bottom, the snow scooter was waiting, its engine already running and the roar of the motor barely audible over the storm. Arjun wasted no time securing Raghav onto the back of the scooter, strapping him down as carefully as possible while keeping him insulated from the wind. Rathod took the front, gripping the handlebars tightly as he prepared to drive through the storm.

"Let's go," Arjun shouted, climbing onto the back, his eyes darting to Raghav. The soldier's breathing was barely detectable, his pulse weak and thready. Arjun's chest tightened as the snow scooter lurched forward, cutting through the storm.

The journey to the lower post was brutal. The wind lashed at them from all sides, making it nearly impossible to see where they were going. The snow swirled around them, blinding them to the path ahead, and the biting cold seeped into their bones, numbing their bodies and minds.

Rathod drove with fierce determination, his face set with grim concentration as the snow scooter tore through the storm. Every bump and jolt sent a ripple of tension through the stretcher where Raghav lay, but they couldn't afford to slow down. The wind was relentless, biting at their faces like daggers of ice, and the swirling snow made it feel as though they were driving through a white void.

Arjun kept his focus entirely on Raghav, his eyes darting back and forth between the soldier's face and his vital signs. The frostbite was getting worse. Raghav's fingers were a sickly gray, his skin pale and lifeless. His breathing was barely perceptible now, shallow gasps coming in irregular intervals. His pulse was weak, erratic, and fading fast.

Arjun cursed under his breath. He had tried to administer IV fluids back at the post, but now, with the temperature plunging and the wind cutting through the small openings in their gear, the tubing had frozen solid.

"He's slipping," Arjun muttered, mostly to himself, though Rathod must have heard him. The weight of those words settled on his chest like a stone.

Rathod pushed the snow scooter harder, leaning into the wind as they sped across the icy landscape. The lower post wasn't far now, but every second felt like an eternity. The blinding snow, the bone-chilling cold, and the relentless wind were all conspiring against them. Arjun's face was raw from the cold, his fingers numb inside his gloves, but he refused to let go of Raghav's stretcher.

"Hold on, Raghav," Arjun whispered, though he wasn't sure the soldier could hear him. "Just hold on a little longer."

The path was uneven, the snow thick in places, and Rathod had to navigate through hidden ridges and patches of ice that threatened to throw them off course. More than once, the snow scooter skidded, nearly losing its grip on the icy ground, but Rathod kept them steady, his eyes fixed on the horizon.

Reaching the Lower Post

Finally, after what felt like hours, they reached the post. It was a small, rugged building nestled into the side of the glacier, with barely enough room for the men stationed there to shelter from the elements. But it was a haven compared to the unforgiving cold outside, and for Arjun, it was their only hope of saving Raghav.

The moment they pulled up to the lower post, soldiers rushed out to help, their faces pinched with concern as they saw the stretcher strapped to the back of the snow scooter. Arjun jumped off, his legs trembling from the cold and exhaustion, and began barking orders.

"Get him inside! We need to get him warmed up and stabilized before the chopper arrives!" His voice was hoarse, his throat dry from the cold air.

The soldiers moved quickly, lifting Raghav off the stretcher and carrying him into the small infirmary inside the post. The room was cramped, with barely enough space for the equipment, but the heater was on full blast, and the temperature was blessedly warm compared to the outside. They laid Raghav on a cot, and Arjun immediately began working, hooking him up to inotropes to stabilize his heart rate.

His fingers were shaking as he worked, the frostbite from the journey making it difficult to move his hands. The

IV fluids finally began to flow, and Raghav's pulse steadied slightly, but his body was still dangerously cold, and the frostbite on his fingers and toes was worsening.

"Is the helicopter on its way?" Arjun asked, his voice tight with urgency as he looked over at the soldiers gathered around.

One of the men nodded. "Yes, sir. We've heard from base camp. The storm's clearing enough for them to send the chopper. It should be here in twenty minutes."

Arjun felt a small flicker of hope, but it was quickly overshadowed by the gravity of the situation. "We don't have much time," he muttered to himself as he continued to work. He checked Raghav's pulse again—stronger now, but still dangerously low. The frostbite had taken hold of his extremities, and Arjun knew that even if Raghav survived, he would likely lose some of his fingers and toes.

The soldiers moved around the small infirmary, preparing for the helicopter's arrival. Rathod and Iyer, their faces pale from the cold and exhaustion, stood silently by the door, watching as Arjun worked. There was little they could do now but wait and hope the helicopter arrived in time.

Waiting for the Helicopter

The minutes crawled by. Outside, the storm was still raging, though it had lessened enough for the helicopter to make its approach. Inside the small infirmary, the tension was palpable. Every sound, every creak of the walls, seemed amplified in the silence. Arjun stood by Raghav's side, his hand resting lightly on the soldier's shoulder as he monitored his vitals.

Raghav's breathing was still shallow, but the inotropes had stabilized his heart rate for now. His body was weak, battered by the cold, and the blood clot in his brain still threatened to end his life at any moment.

Rathod spoke up, his voice low. "Do you think he'll make it, Doc?"

Arjun didn't answer right away. He looked down at Raghav, the young soldier's face gaunt and pale, his body wrapped in layers of blankets to fend off the cold. "I don't know," he said finally, his voice heavy with uncertainty. "It depends on how fast we can get him to proper care. The frostbite's bad, and the clot… I'm not sure if we've stabilized it enough."

Iyer shifted uncomfortably, his eyes fixed on the small window where the storm still raged outside. "I've never seen anyone this bad off. Do we know what's going to happen if they don't get here in time?"

Arjun hesitated, his throat tightening. "If they don't get here in time, we'll lose him."

The words hung in the air, a stark reminder of the stakes. Outside, the sound of the wind howled, but inside, the silence was suffocating. Every soldier in the room understood the weight of what was happening. They had seen their share of death on the glacier, but this was different. This was a battle not with guns or enemies, but with nature itself—a battle they were fighting minute by minute, hoping for a miracle.

Suddenly, the low, distant thrum of helicopter blades cut through the silence. Arjun's heart leapt in his chest, and he turned toward the window. The faint glow of the helicopter's lights was barely visible through the snow, but it was enough.

"They're here!" Rathod shouted, and the soldiers sprang into action.

Arjun grabbed his medical bag and rushed toward the door, his heart racing. The helicopter was their last chance to save Raghav, and he wasn't about to let it slip away.

The Helicopter's Arrival

The helicopter touched down in a swirl of snow and wind, the rotor blades cutting through the air with a deafening roar. The soldiers shielded their faces from the blast of cold air as they hurried toward the aircraft, carrying Raghav on the stretcher.

Arjun followed closely, his hands trembling from the cold and adrenaline as they loaded Raghav into the helicopter. The medical team onboard was already waiting, and one of the doctors, bundled in thick gear, immediately took charge of the situation.

"What's his status?" the doctor shouted over the noise of the rotors as he began checking Raghav's vitals.

"Severe frostbite, CVT, and hypoxia. He's been stable for the last twenty minutes, but he's slipping. Inotropes have kept his heart rate up, but we're losing ground," Arjun replied, his voice tight with urgency.

The doctor nodded quickly, his face focused. "We'll take it from here."

The helicopter's engine roared to life, and Arjun watched as it lifted off, disappearing into the swirling storm. The noise of the rotors faded into the distance, leaving only the howling wind behind.

Sharma appeared beside him, his face weary but relieved. "They'll get him to the base hospital in time, Doc. You did everything you could."

Arjun nodded, though his mind was still racing. "I hope so. But we're not out of the woods yet."

Arrival at Base Camp

The helicopter landed at base camp amidst a flurry of snow, the rotors kicking up clouds of ice and powder. The medical team on the ground rushed out, ready to transport Raghav from the helicopter to the hospital. Tension hung in the air as they moved quickly, wheeling the stretcher through the snow and into the warmer confines of the medical facility.

Inside the hospital, a team of doctors and nurses waited, already alerted to the emergency by the post team. Raghav's heart had stabilized for the moment, but his condition remained critical. The frostbite had worsened, and his body temperature was dangerously low. The next step was prepping him for immediate transfer to Chandigarh, where a more advanced medical team could address the blood clot and frostbite damage.

The helicopter doctor handed over Raghav's medical notes to the hospital team, his tone brisk yet thorough. "We stabilized him, but he's still critical. Severe frostbite to the extremities, CVT, and hypoxia. His heart's weak, but we've kept him going with inotropes."

The base camp doctor nodded grimly. "We'll prep him for transfer right away. The airlift to Chandigarh is set to go as soon as he's stable for flight. It's touch-and-go."

He stepped back, watching as the base team efficiently took over. They worked together like a well-oiled machine, hooking Raghav up to advanced equipment, stabilizing him for the next leg of the journey.

The Final Race to Chandigarh

Back at the lower post, Arjun sat with his hands clasped tightly in front of him, anxiously waiting for news. The radio crackled intermittently, but no update has come yet. Time seemed to stretch out endlessly, each minute dragging as he imagined the scene unfolding at base camp. Was Raghav still alive? Had they stabilized him? Every possible scenario played out in his mind, none offering relief.

Sharma returned from outside, rubbing his hands together, shaking the snow from his coat before sitting across from Arjun. "Still no word?" he asked.

Arjun shook his head. "Nothing. They should be at base camp by now."

"They will be," Sharma replied, his voice steady. "Raghav's tough. He'll pull through."

But even Sharma's reassuring words couldn't shake the gnawing worry in Arjun's gut. He stood abruptly, pacing in front of the small window. Outside, the storm had eased, though the wind still rattled the walls. The snow was falling lightly now, settling into a soft blanket over the harsh terrain.

Suddenly, the sharp crackle of the radio broke the silence. Arjun froze, his heart skipping a beat as Dr. Singh's voice came through the static.

"Base camp to lower post. This is Dr. Singh. We've stabilized Raghav for now. He's being prepped for airlift to Chandigarh. His condition's still critical, but he's holding on. We've got him on life support and are doing everything we can. Over."

Arjun exhaled a breath he hadn't realized he was holding, his hands gripping the radio tightly. The message was a glimmer of hope, but far from a victory. Raghav was stable for the moment, but the real challenge lay ahead in Chandigarh, where specialists would have to deal with the cerebral venous thrombosis (CVT) and frostbite.

"Roger, Dr. Singh. Thanks for the update," Arjun replied, his voice steadier than he felt. "Keep us informed when he's in the air. Over."

The crackle faded, and silence fell over the room once more. Arjun slumped into the nearest chair, staring blankly at the radio. He could picture the scene at base camp: doctors working around Raghav, hooking him up to machines, monitoring his fragile vitals as they prepared him for the journey to Chandigarh.

Sharma, sitting across from him, offered a sympathetic look. "The hard part's out of your hands now, Captain."

"I know," Arjun muttered, rubbing his face. He hadn't realized just how drained he was until that moment. His fingers were stiff from the cold, and his muscles ached from the tension. He leaned back, staring at the ceiling. "I just… I feel I should be there. I know Singh and his team are more than capable, but…"

Sharma finished his thought. "It's never easy when you've been fighting for someone's life. You're invested. But you've done more than most could. You gave him a chance."

Arjun sighed, letting Sharma's words sink in. He was right. He had done everything he could on the ice wall, battling the elements and time to keep Raghav alive. But still, it was hard to let go, especially with the outcome so uncertain.

The Airlift to Chandigarh

At base camp, the helicopter was being prepared for the final, critical flight. Raghav had been stabilized, but the toll on his body was clear. The frostbite had ravaged his extremities, and his pulse was still weak. The medical team worked swiftly, ensuring he was ready for the flight to Chandigarh.

Dr. Singh stayed close, overseeing every detail as the helicopter was refueled and prepped. The airlift was their best shot at saving Raghav's life. The base camp medical team had done all they could with their limited resources. In Chandigarh, a full critical care team awaited, equipped to perform the delicate surgery needed to dissolve the clot and treat the frostbite.

Singh checked Raghav's vitals once more. His heart rate was still irregular, and the frostbite was severe. Singh glanced at another doctor on his team. "We'll need to watch him closely during the flight."

The other doctor nodded grimly. "The defibrillator's ready, and the portable ventilator is secure. Let's hope we make it there without another emergency."

With everything in place, Raghav was loaded onto the helicopter, and the team climbed aboard, their faces set in concentration. The rotors spun up, and Dr. Singh took a deep breath. This was the last leg of the journey, the most critical. They had done everything they could to keep Raghav stable, but it was clear that the young soldier was still on the edge of life and death.

The helicopter lifted off, the snow-covered base camp falling away beneath them. Inside, the medical team worked in near silence, the hum of the machines and the beeping of the heart monitor the only sounds breaking the tension. Raghav's survival now depended on the skill of the doctors waiting in Chandigarh—and on making it there in time.

Cardiac Arrest in the Air

Halfway through the flight, the worst happened. The heart monitor's steady beeping faltered, then escalated into a frantic alarm. Dr. Pritam's head snapped up.

"Cardiac arrest!" Pritam shouted, immediately springing into action. His team moved quickly, administering chest compressions while another team member readied the defibrillator.

The helicopter jolted as they hit a patch of turbulence, but the medical team remained focused. Raghav's body jolted with the first shock from the defibrillator, but the monitor showed no change. Pritam wiped the sweat from his brow, despite the cold, and ordered a second shock.

"Come on, Raghav," Pritam muttered under his breath as they administered the second shock. The heart monitor beeped again, this time with a weak but regular rhythm.

"He's back," one team member said, though the relief was muted. They had to get him to Chandigarh, and fast.

The minutes ticked by slowly as the helicopter sped toward its destination. Pritam kept his eyes glued to the monitor, his hand on Raghav's pulse, ready to spring into action at the first sign of trouble.

At last, the lights of Chandigarh appeared, a beacon of hope piercing the dark sky. The helicopter began its descent, and Singh allowed himself a small breath of relief. They had made it.

On the ground, the trauma team at the Chandigarh hospital was waiting. As soon as the helicopter touched down, the doors were flung open, and Raghav was rushed out on a stretcher, surrounded by doctors and nurses. Pritam followed close behind, shouting updates on Raghav's condition as they wheeled him into the critical care unit.

"He's had one cardiac arrest, severe frostbite, and CVT. We stabilized him in the air, but his vitals are still weak. He needs immediate intervention," Pritam explained as they hurried down the hallway.

The lead doctor, Colonel Ramchandra, nodded. "We're ready. We'll start with the clot removal. The frostbite will have to wait."

Pritam watched as Raghav was wheeled into the building, his body pale and fragile beneath layers of blankets. The doors swung shut, leaving Pritam and his team standing in silence, the weight of the journey finally sinking in.

The Waiting Game

Back at the lower post, Arjun and Sharma sat in tense silence, their faces illuminated by the faint glow of the heater. Each hour since the helicopter's departure had felt like an eternity as they waited for any news from Chandigarh.

The radio sat on the table between them, silent and foreboding. Every instinct in Arjun wanted to be there, in Chandigarh, seeing the fight through to the end.

"Captain," Sharma said softly, breaking the silence. "You need to rest."

Arjun shook his head, his eyes bloodshot from exhaustion. "I can't. Not until I know he's out of danger."

Sharma didn't push him. He knew Arjun too well. Silence stretched between them again, interrupted only by the sound of the storm outside, now less intense but still present—a reminder of how little control they had over the situation.

Inside the operating room, Dr. Ramachandra and his team worked with expert precision. The clot in Raghav's brain was large and dangerously close to causing irreversible damage, and the frostbite complicated matters. Every second mattered as they delicately removed the clot, restoring proper blood flow.

"Clot's out," Dr. Ramachandra finally announced, his voice steady but tense. "But he's still critical."

The frostbite damage was severe, and the team knew some of Raghav's extremities might be beyond saving. But for now, the focus was on stabilizing him—on giving him the best chance at survival.

The Radio Call

Hours passed before the radio at the lower post crackled to life. Arjun bolted upright, grabbing the radio with trembling hands.

"This is Colonel Ramachandra from Chandigarh," the voice came through, clear but tired. "Raghav's out of surgery.

We removed the clot, but his condition is still critical. He's stable for now, but the frostbite has caused severe damage. We'll be monitoring him closely for the next 24 hours."

Arjun exhaled slowly, his hands shaking with relief. They had made it. Raghav was alive.

"Thank you, Sir," Arjun said into the radio, his voice thick with emotion. "Thank you."

After a brief pause, Colonel replied. "You saved him, Captain. We just took over where you left off. You gave him a fighting chance."

The radio crackled once more and fell silent. Arjun remained seated, his head hanging low as the weight of everything settled over him. The adrenaline had kept him going, but now that it was over, he felt utterly drained.

Sharma, standing beside him, gave him a firm pat on the shoulder. "You gave him a second chance, Captain. You've done all you can. Now, get some rest."

Arjun nodded, though rest still felt impossible. Raghav was still in critical condition, teetering on the edge of survival. The procedure was just one battle—the next 24 hours would decide whether he would live through the aftermath of frostbite, hypoxia, and the trauma his body had endured.

Reflection at the Glacier

Arjun found himself standing at the edge of the ice wall, staring out across the frozen expanse, his mind replaying the events of the past days over and over again.

The silence of the glacier was both oppressive and peaceful. It reminded him of the fragility of life in such a brutal environment, but also of the resilience it took to survive here. Each day on the glacier was a battle—not just against the cold or the altitude, but against the slow erosion of the spirit, the isolation, and the constant threat of death.

Rathod and Iyer Joined him, standing silently by his side. None of them spoke for a long time, the memory of Raghav's rescue still fresh in their minds. The descent down the ice wall, the fierce storm, the desperate race to the lower post, and the long wait for news from Chandigarh had left them all with a shared sense of both relief and exhaustion.

"Doc," Rathod finally spoke, breaking the silence, "you think he's going to be okay?"

Arjun kept his gaze fixed on the horizon, his breath visible in the cold air. "He'll make it," he replied, though his voice was quiet and thoughtful. "But it's going to be a long road for him. He's got a lot of recovery ahead."

Iyer exhaled heavily, his hands buried deep in his jacket pockets. "He's lucky. To survive all of that…"

Arjun nodded slowly, the weight of the truth settling over him. "Yeah. He is."

The glacier, vast and unmoving, seemed indifferent to the drama that had played out on its surface. It would continue to claim victims, continue to test the limits of those who dared to stand on it. But for now, in this moment, Arjun felt a quiet sense of victory. They had won this battle—Raghav had survived—and in this harsh, frozen land, that was no small feat.

A Letter from Chandigarh

Weeks later, as the routine of the post continued and the glacier returned to its cold, indifferent self, a letter arrived from Chandigarh. It was addressed to Captain Arjun, and the moment he saw the envelope, his heart skipped a beat.

He opened it carefully, his fingers trembling slightly as he pulled out the letter inside. It was from Colonel Ramachandra.

Captain Arjun,

I wanted to personally update you on Naik Raghav's progress. He's doing remarkably well, considering everything he's been through. His frostbite injuries required the amputation of several fingers and toes, but he's in good spirits and eager to begin his rehabilitation. The clot in his brain has been fully resolved, and he's regained most of his cognitive functions.

Raghav asked me to pass along a message to you: 'Thank you for saving my life.' He knows how close he came to not making it, and he's incredibly grateful for everything you did.

I'll keep you updated on his recovery. It will be a long journey, but I have no doubt that he'll come through stronger than before.

Best regards,
Colonel Ramachandra

Arjun read the letter twice, a slow smile spreading across his face. He had done it. Raghav had made it through, and despite everything, he had survived. The glacier had tested them all, pushing them to their limits, but they had won this battle. For the first time in weeks, Arjun felt a sense of peace settle over him.

He folded the letter carefully and tucked it into his jacket, feeling the warmth of the sun on his face as he stepped outside. The glacier stretched out before him, vast and unyielding, but today, it felt a little less hostile.

And for now, that was enough.

Chapter 6

THE GLACIER'S FURY

Life at Post - Struggling with Daily Survival

The barracks themselves were little more than a collection of prefabricated huts huddled together in the middle of this frozen wasteland. Inside, the soldiers moved quietly, their faces lined with exhaustion and weariness. There were only a handful of them stationed here, and they were all fighting the same battle—not against an enemy they could see, but against the glacier itself. It was an unyielding, indifferent adversary, one that tested them every single day.

Arjun rubbed his hands together, trying to ward off the cold that had found its way into his bones. Despite the layers of clothing, the thick gloves, and the heaters that hummed weakly in the corner, the cold was omnipresent. It was in the air, in the walls, in every breath he took.

Lieutenant Iyer, sat nearby flipping through a book he had read at least five times already. His face was gaunt, his eyes hollowed from lack of sleep. No one at the post slept well. The wind, always howling, made the barracks creak and groan through the night, and the temperature inside never rose above what could generously be described as "chilly."

"You ever get tired of the cold?" Iyer asked, not looking up from his book.

Arjun smiled faintly, though there was no humor in it. "Every day."

The food situation wasn't helping. Supplies were running low, and the weather had been too unpredictable for the regular helicopter drop. They were down to the last of their rations, and even those were being stretched thin.

Iyer stood up, crossing the small room to the makeshift kitchen area, where Verma was trying to prepare what little food they had left. Verma, always resourceful, had managed to stretch the last of the eggs into something resembling a meal, though it was hardly appetizing.

"Boiling eggs in a pressure cooker," Verma muttered, shaking his head. "Never thought I'd see the day."

Arjun joined them, peering over Verma's shoulder. The eggs, barely cooked, floated in a pot of lukewarm water. The stove, running on what little fuel they had left, struggled to maintain enough heat to even bring the water to a full boil. The pressure cooker hissed and sputtered, but it was barely enough.

"It's the altitude," Iyer said, leaning against the counter. "You need more heat to boil water properly up here. Without enough fuel, it's like trying to cook with a candle."

Verma nodded grimly. "At this rate, we'll be eating raw eggs for dinner."

Arjun laughed, though it came out more a short, tired breath. "Better than nothing."

The men fell silent, the weight of the situation settling over them once again. They all knew the reality of their situation. If the supply helicopter didn't arrive soon, they'd be down to emergency rations—tasteless, barely-nutritional packets designed for survival, not sustenance. And even those wouldn't last long.

"You know," Verma said after a moment, stirring the pot of eggs, "my mother used to make eggs for breakfast every morning. Fried, scrambled, boiled—didn't matter. Always cooked perfectly."

Iyer grinned. "Bet she didn't have to use a pressure cooker."

Verma shook his head, a small smile tugging at the corners of his mouth. "No, she didn't."

The conversation drifted after that, the men lapsing into silence once more. It was hard to keep the conversation going when every thought seemed to circle back to the same concerns—the cold, the isolation, the dwindling supplies. They were trapped here, at the mercy of the glacier, and there was nothing they could do but wait.

The Storm Approaches

The sky had been ominous for days, thick clouds rolling in from the west, casting the glacier in a pale, eerie light. Arjun could sense the change in the air, the storm building like a beast ready to pounce. The wind had picked up, and the temperature had dropped even further.

Major Sharma had been monitoring the weather reports, but they were always unpredictable at this altitude. A storm could come out of nowhere, hitting them with full force before they even had time to prepare.

The men gathered in the briefing room that morning, their breath visible in the freezing air, as Sharma outlined the plan.

"The supply helicopter is scheduled to arrive at 1400 hours," Sharma said, his voice steady but laced with tension. "This storm is moving fast, and we don't have much time. We'll need to clear the landing zone and make sure the signal flares are ready. The helicopter won't have much time to land, so we need to be quick and precise."

Arjun nodded along with the others, mentally preparing for the tasks ahead. Supply drops were always critical, but in conditions like this, they were even more dangerous. The storm was already beginning to pick up speed, the wind howling outside the thin walls of the briefing room. Visibility would be near zero by the time the helicopter arrived, and they had no margin for error.

"We'll split into teams," Sharma continued, his eyes scanning the room. "Iyer and Verma take the flares and position yourselves at the north and south ends of the landing zone. Arjun and I will handle communications and make sure the landing area is cleared of snow. We'll have to move fast."

The men dispersed to gather their gear, the tension in the air palpable. There was no room for mistakes—without the supplies, they wouldn't last much longer. The rations were nearly gone, and the heaters were running low on fuel. This drop was their lifeline.

Outside, the wind had picked up even more, whipping snow into their faces as they trudged through the knee-deep drifts toward the landing zone. The cold was unforgiving, the kind that cut straight through you, no matter how many layers you wore. Arjun could barely feel his fingers, even through his thick gloves.

Iyer and Verma moved quickly, setting up the flares at the designated points, their faces wrapped in scarves and goggles to shield them from the biting wind. Troops worked to clear the landing area, shoveling the snow as fast as they could, though it felt like a losing battle. Every time they cleared a patch, the wind would blow more snow back into place.

"This storm's going to hit us hard," Sharma shouted over the wind, his voice barely audible. "We need to be ready for anything."

Arjun nodded, his eyes scanning the horizon for any sign of the helicopter. He could hear the faint thrum of the rotors in the distance, but the visibility was so poor he couldn't make out anything beyond a few feet. The snow was coming down in thick sheets now, swirling around them in blinding gusts.

"Here they come!" Iyer's voice crackled through the radio, cutting through the wind. "I can see them approaching from the west."

Arjun strained his eyes, trying to make out the shape of the helicopter through the storm. The sound of the rotors grew louder, but the aircraft was barely visible, just a dark shadow moving through the swirling snow.

The pilot was struggling to keep the helicopter steady, the wind battering the aircraft from all sides. It wobbled in the air, its rotors slicing through the storm, but it seemed they were going to make it.

But then, in an instant, everything went wrong.

A sudden gust of wind, stronger than anything they had felt before, caught the helicopter's tail rotor, spinning the aircraft wildly out of control. Arjun watched in horror as the helicopter tilted to one side, the rotors dangerously close to the ground.

"Get back!" Sharma shouted, his voice urgent.

The men scattered, diving for cover as the helicopter veered dangerously off course. The tail rotor smashed into a snowbank, the sound of the crash deafening as metal screeched against ice. The helicopter lurched, then slammed into the ground with a force that sent a shockwave through the glacier.

Arjun scrambled to his feet, his heart pounding in his chest. The helicopter lay on its side, half-buried in snow, the rotors still spinning slowly as the engine sputtered and died. For a moment, there was nothing but the howling wind and the eerie silence that followed the crash.

"Is anyone alive in there?" Verma shouted, his voice frantic as he rushed toward the wreckage.

Arjun followed, his boots sinking into the snow with every step. He could see movement inside the cockpit, the pilot struggling to free himself from the tangled mess of straps and controls.

"Help me!" the pilot's voice was muffled by the storm, but Arjun could hear the desperation in his tone.

He reached the helicopter at the same time as Iyer, and together they pulled open the twisted metal door. Inside, the pilot was covered in blood, his face pale from shock and the cold. His co-pilot lay slumped in his seat, unconscious but breathing.

"We need to get them out of here!" Arjun shouted over the wind.

Together, he and Iyer dragged the pilot and co-pilot from the wreckage, the wind pushing against them with relentless force. It felt like they were fighting against the glacier itself, every step a battle as they made their way toward the safety of the barracks.

The storm was unrelenting, the snow coming down in blinding sheets, but somehow, they made it inside. The warmth of the barracks hit them like a wall, though it was barely above freezing inside. The men worked quickly to lay the injured pilots on the cots, checking their vitals, doing what they could to stabilize them.

"He's got a broken leg," Iyer muttered, his voice tight with concern as he examined the co-pilot. "It's bad. We need to splint it before he goes into shock."

Arjun grabbed the medical kit and worked with Iyer to splint the co-pilot's leg, his hands shaking from the cold and the adrenaline. The pilot, though conscious, was in no better shape. His face was pale, and he groaned in pain with every breath.

"We need to get them out of here," Sharma said, already on the radio, trying to contact command. "This storm's only getting worse."

The Rescue Effort

The radio crackled with static as Major Sharma attempted to reach command, his voice steady despite the chaos around him. The storm outside was raging, and the barracks felt small and claustrophobic with the weight of the crisis bearing down on them. The injured pilots lay on the makeshift cots, their faces pale, their breaths shallow.

Arjun stood by the window, watching the storm batter the thin walls of Post Zero. His mind raced, trying to process the events of the last hour. The crash, the rescue, the injuries—they had all happened so fast, but now came the waiting. They needed help, and fast, but with the storm bearing down on them, there was no telling when—or if—it would come.

"We need an evac as soon as possible," Sharma said into the radio, his voice tense. "We've got two injured—one critical. We're doing what we can to stabilize them, but we need medical support."

The response from command was faint, barely audible through the static. "Understood, Major. We're working on sending a rescue team, but the storm's making it difficult. It could be hours before they reach you. Hold tight."

Sharma set the radio down, his face grim as he turned to Arjun. "We're on our own for now."

Arjun nodded, the weight of the situation settling over him like a blanket of snow. The storm outside was unrelenting, and they were miles away from the nearest base with full medical facilities. It was up to them to keep the pilots alive until help could arrive.

The Fight Against Time

The hours dragged on, the storm outside intensifying with each passing minute. Inside the barracks, the air was thick with tension as the men worked tirelessly to keep the injured pilots alive. The temperature had dropped even further, and the barracks, though insulated, were barely keeping the cold at bay.

Iyer had taken over monitoring the co-pilot, whose leg had been splinted, but his condition was deteriorating. The man's breathing had become more labored, and his skin had taken on a bluish tint—signs of shock. Verma worked on the pilot, doing his best to keep him conscious and alert, but the pilot's injuries were severe. Arjun knew that without immediate medical intervention, both men could slip away.

"We need to keep them warm," Arjun said, his voice low but firm. "The cold's only going to make things worse. We're not losing them to hypothermia on top of everything else."

Sharma nodded, already moving toward the stove to stoke the small fire they had going.

"We can use the thermal blankets from the emergency kit," Verma suggested, grabbing one from a nearby shelf. "Wrap them up tight. It'll help."

Arjun and Iyer worked together, carefully wrapping the injured men in the blankets, trying to trap what little body heat they had left. The co-pilot's pulse was weak, his eyelids fluttering as he fought to stay conscious. Arjun could feel the man's life slipping away, and it terrified him.

"We need to keep talking to them," Arjun said, his voice strained. "If they pass out, it's going to be harder to bring them back."

Verma knelt beside the pilot, gently shaking his shoulder. "Stay with us, buddy. Don't fall asleep."

The pilot groaned in response, his eyes barely open. "Hurts… everything hurts," he muttered, his words slurred.

"I know," Verma said softly. "But you've got to hang on. Help's on the way."

But was it? Arjun glanced toward Sharma, who had just finished speaking with command again. The major's face told him everything he needed to know.

"The storm's grounding the rescue helicopter," Sharma said quietly. "They're going to try again in the morning if the weather clears. We're on our own until then."

A heavy silence fell over the room. Morning felt a lifetime away, and the storm showed no signs of relenting. The realization that they were truly alone sank in, and for a moment, Arjun felt the crushing weight of the glacier pressing down on him. They had survived the crash, but now, survival was an hour-by-hour struggle.

"We'll make it through," Sharma said, his voice cutting through the silence. "We just have to keep them stable. Keep them warm, keep their vitals in check. We can do this."

Arjun nodded, forcing himself to focus. This wasn't the time to give in to fear. They had made it this far, and they would make it through the night, no matter how bleak things seemed.

Food and Survival

Hours passed, and the men rotated in shifts, tending to the injured and trying to maintain some semblance of warmth. The barracks were cold, the small fire in the stove barely making a dent in the biting chill that seeped through the walls. The storm continued to howl outside, the wind rattling the windows and doors.

At some point during the night, Arjun's stomach growled, reminding him that it had been hours since they'd eaten anything. They had been so focused on keeping the pilots alive that they had neglected their own basic needs.

"We need to eat something," Iyer said, breaking the silence. "We're no good to them if we collapse from hunger."

Arjun sighed, the weight of Iyer's words sinking in. "You're right," he said, rubbing his eyes. The exhaustion and cold had dulled their senses, but hunger gnawed at them now, demanding attention. They hadn't eaten anything substantial in hours, and the bitter cold only intensified the need for calories.

The mention of food reminded everyone of the painful reality: the helicopter crash that had brought hope also left them with shattered supplies scattered across the glacier, now mostly useless. The helicopter had been their lifeline, the one thing they had counted on to bring them much-needed supplies.

Verma, seated next to the heater, sighed in frustration. "The irony, huh? We finally get a supply drop, and it crashes right in front of us. Even the damned food got wrecked."

Arjun nodded grimly. The wreckage of the helicopter still haunted his thoughts. He remembered how, in the chaos of the crash, they had raced to pull out the injured pilots and stabilize them. Amidst that frenzy, no one had paid much attention to the scattered boxes that had fallen with the helicopter—boxes that were supposed to contain food, fuel, and essentials they so desperately needed.

"I checked the boxes," Verma added. "What wasn't smashed to bits is either frozen solid or contaminated. The cans are dented and split open, and half of the perishables are gone."

Arjun clenched his jaw. He had seen the carnage earlier when they'd attempted to salvage whatever they could from the wreckage. Food supplies—biscuits, canned beans, dried fruit—had been crushed under the helicopter's weight or ruined by the extreme cold. A large tin of cooking oil had burst open, spilling its contents over other supplies, rendering everything slick and inedible. Some of the few intact food items had frozen so solidly they might as well have been rocks.

Sharma nodded in agreement. "What do we have left in the supplies?

Arjun headed to the small cupboard where they kept their remaining rations. The supply situation had been dire even before the helicopter crash, and now they were down to the bare essentials. The only thing they had in any significant quantity was eggs—cases of them, meant to last until the next supply drop.

"Eggs," Arjun said with a sigh, holding up one of the cartons. "Looks like we're going to be boiling eggs again."

"Great," Verma muttered, his voice laced with sarcasm. "Nothing like boiled eggs in a snowstorm to lift your spirits."

Iyer chuckled softly, though the sound was tired. "Better than nothing."

They filled a pressure cooker with water and set it on the small stove, waiting for it to heat up. The process was slow, the weak fire barely able to bring the water to a boil. When the eggs were finally ready, they handed them out in silence, each man cracking the shells and eating with mechanical efficiency.

Arjun couldn't help but think about how surreal the situation was—sitting in a freezing barracks, surrounded by injured men, eating boiled eggs while a storm raged outside. It felt like some twisted survival experiment, a test of their endurance and willpower.

As they ate, Sharma spoke up, his voice quiet but resolute. "We're going to get through this. We've faced worse."

"Have we?" Verma asked, raising an eyebrow. "Because I don't remember the last time we had to deal with a helicopter crash in the middle of a blizzard."

Sharma shrugged. "Maybe not this exact situation, but we've been in tight spots before. We're soldiers. We adapt, we survive."

Arjun nodded in agreement, though part of him wondered if they were reaching the limits of what they could adapt to.

"One step at a time," Arjun said, echoing the words that had become their mantra over the last few days. "We just have to get through tonight."

The Long Night

The night dragged on, each minute feeling like an hour as the storm continued to batter the post. The barracks creaked under the weight of the wind, and the snow piled up outside, threatening to bury them completely. Inside, the men huddled near the stove, taking turns checking on the injured pilots.

The co-pilot's condition had worsened, his pulse weakening despite their best efforts to keep him warm and stable. His skin had turned a pale, bluish color, and his breathing was shallow. Arjun had done everything he could—splinted the leg, administered painkillers, and kept him as comfortable as possible—but there was only so much they could do with the limited supplies they had.

"He's not going to make it through the night," Verma whispered, his voice filled with a quiet resignation. "We're losing him."

Arjun clenched his jaw, his mind racing for solutions, but there were none. They were cut off from the outside world, their only hope of survival resting on a rescue helicopter that might not come in time.

"Keep talking to him," Arjun said, his voice tight. "Don't let him slip away."

Verma nodded, moving closer to the co-pilot and gently shaking his shoulder. "Hey, stay with us, okay? You're not alone."

The co-pilot's eyes fluttered open for a moment, his gaze unfocused. He mumbled something unintelligible before his eyes slid shut again.

Arjun felt a surge of frustration. They were so close to losing him, and there was nothing they could do to stop it. The helplessness gnawed at him, but he pushed it down. He couldn't afford to give in to despair—not when the others were depending on him to keep it together.

Iyer, who had been sitting quietly by the stove, spoke up. "The storm's not going to last forever. We just have to make it through."

Arjun nodded, though the words felt hollow. The storm might end, but their problems wouldn't. Even if the rescue helicopter came in the morning, there was no guarantee the pilots would survive the trip back to base. And then there was the issue of their own dwindling supplies—how long could they hold out before the glacier claimed them too?

Sharma, ever the steady presence, stood up and began pacing the room. "We've made it this far. We're not giving up now. The helicopter will come. We just have to keep fighting."

Arjun watched him, grateful for his unwavering resolve. Sharma had always been the one to keep them focused, to remind them of their duty when things got tough. But even he couldn't deny that they were running out of options.

The hours crept by, and the storm showed no signs of letting up. Arjun dozed fitfully in his chair, the cold and exhaustion weighing heavily on him. Every time he closed his eyes, he saw flashes of the helicopter crashing into the snow, the rotors spinning wildly as the aircraft tilted. The sound of metal grinding against ice echoed in his ears, followed by the deafening silence that had come afterward.

When he opened his eyes again, the barracks were still. The only sound was the faint crackle of the stove, and the rhythmic breathing of the men around him. Iyer and Verma had fallen asleep, their bodies slumped against the wall, while Sharma sat by the window, keeping watch.

Arjun stood up and stretched, his muscles stiff from hours of sitting in the cold. He walked over to the injured pilots, checking their vitals once more. The co-pilot's condition hadn't improved, but he was still hanging on—barely.

"We're going to make it through," Arjun whispered, though he wasn't sure who he was trying to convince—the pilots or himself.

The Morning After

When dawn finally broke, the storm had subsided, leaving behind a world blanketed in snow. The wind had died down, and the air outside was eerily still, as if the glacier itself were holding its breath. The men stirred from their makeshift beds, their bodies stiff and aching from the cold.

Sharma was the first to move, heading to the radio to check in with command. Arjun followed, his heart pounding in his chest as they waited for a response. The crackle of static filled the room, and for a moment, it seemed they were still cut off from the outside world. But then, a faint voice came through.

"This is command. Rescue helicopter is en route. ETA thirty minutes. How are the injured?"

Arjun exchanged a glance with Sharma before responding. "We've stabilized them as best we can, but the co-pilot's in critical condition. We need that helicopter here now."

"Understood," the voice on the other end said. "We're moving as fast as we can. Hang tight."

The next thirty minutes felt like an eternity. The men moved in a flurry of activity, preparing the pilots for extraction and clearing a path to the landing zone. The snow was deep, but the skies were clear, and for the first time in what felt like days, there was a sense of hope in the air.

When the sound of the helicopter's rotors finally reached their ears, it was a welcome relief. The aircraft appeared on the horizon, cutting through the crisp morning air, its bright lights shining like a beacon of salvation.

The rescue team moved quickly, lifting the injured pilots into the helicopter and securing them for transport. Arjun watched as they worked, his body tense with exhaustion and relief. They had made it through the night. They had survived.

As the helicopter lifted off, taking the pilots back to safety, Arjun stood with the others, watching it disappear into the sky. The storm had passed, and they had made it through—together.

But as they trudged back to the barracks, the weight of what they had endured settled over them. The glacier had tested them, pushed them to their limits, and though they had survived this battle, they knew there would be more challenges ahead.

Surviving on the Glacier's Rations

After the rescue helicopter faded into the horizon, the men returned to the barracks with a grim sense of victory. They had saved the pilots, but the storm had taken its toll—not just on their bodies, but on their supplies. The realization hit hard as Arjun opened the cupboard to find it practically bare.

"What's left?" Sharma asked, his voice flat as he pulled off his gloves and rubbed his stiff hands together to warm them.

Arjun frowned, his eyes scanning the meager contents. "Not much," he admitted. "We've got a few more cartons of eggs, some rice, dried lentils, and tea. Everything else is either gone or frozen solid."

Sharma let out a weary sigh, running a hand over his face. "We'll have to make do until the next supply drop," he muttered. "When's that?"

Verma, who had been cleaning his rifle near the small heater, glanced up. "Could be weeks," he said, his tone resigned. "With the weather, there's no guarantee when the next chopper can make it through."

The men exchanged glances, the gravity of the situation sinking in. The cold and isolation had always been the glacier's worst weapons, but now, hunger was creeping into the equation. The thought of living off nothing but eggs, rice, and lentils for the foreseeable future didn't exactly inspire confidence.

Arjun tried to lighten the mood. "Well, at least we've got eggs," he said with a forced smile. "Plenty of ways to cook eggs, right?"

Verma snorted. "Boiled, fried, scrambled. Doesn't really matter when you're sick of them all."

Iyer, sitting at the far end of the room, spoke up with a smirk. "We can always get creative. How about egg curry? We've got the lentils, and I'm sure we can figure something out."

Arjun raised an eyebrow. "Okay, Whatever."

Sharma, despite the dire circumstances, chuckled. "It might be worth a try. Anything to make this a little less miserable."

Cooking on the Glacier

"Does anyone know how to make an omelet properly?" Arjun asked, standing in front of the small stove with the carton of eggs in hand.

"I don't think anyone's concerned about 'proper' right now," Iyer replied, watching as he stirred a pot of lentils for the day's lunch. "Just crack the eggs and throw in whatever we've got."

Arjun followed Iyer's advice, cracking several eggs into a bowl and whisking them together. He added some salt, pepper, and a few crushed red chili flakes from a small jar they had managed to salvage from the supply run weeks ago. He poured the mixture into the pan, watching as it sizzled slightly on the hot surface.

It wasn't much, but it was better than plain boiled eggs again. As he flipped the omelet, he could hear Verma chuckling from across the room.

"What's so funny?" Arjun asked, not taking his eyes off the pan.

"I was just thinking," Verma said, leaning back in his chair. "We're up here, on one of the deadliest glaciers in the world, freezing our asses off, and you're worried about perfecting your omelet."

"Hey, a good omelet can do wonders for morale," Arjun shot back with a grin. "Besides, we've got to make the best of what we've got."

When the omelet was finally ready, Arjun divided it up and handed out small portions to the men. The room fell quiet as they ate, the simple meal providing a brief reprieve from the constant grind of survival.

"Not bad," Iyer said, nodding in approval. "Could use some onions, though. Maybe tomatoes."

"Yeah, and a dash of coriander," Sharma added, though his tone was more wistful than critical.

"Right, because those are in abundance up here," Arjun replied, shaking his head. "Maybe we can plant a garden next to the snowdrift outside."

The men laughed, the humor lightening the otherwise grim mood.

Rationing the Supplies

As the days passed, the reality of their dwindling food supply became impossible to ignore. Despite their best efforts to ration, the cartons of eggs were running low, and they had already used up most of the rice. The dried lentils were still in decent supply, but without fresh ingredients to pair them with, every meal felt like a repeat of the last.

Sharma called a meeting one evening, gathering the men around the small heater that provided the only warmth in the barracks. His face was drawn, his eyes tired from both the cold and the weight of their situation.

"We've got to stretch the food as long as possible," Sharma said, his voice steady but grim. "I know it's not much, but we can't afford to waste anything. No more than two meals a day. We'll supplement with tea when we need to."

Arjun nodded, understanding the logic behind it, but the thought of cutting back even further weighed heavily on him. They were already operating on minimal calories, and with the constant need to maintain the equipment and patrol the perimeter, their bodies were burning through what little energy they had.

"How long until the next supply drop?" Iyer asked, his voice tight with worry.

"Could be a week, maybe two," Sharma replied. "It depends on the weather. We'll manage until then. We have to."

The men nodded in agreement, though the uncertainty hung in the air like a dark cloud. The glacier was unpredictable, and there was no telling when or if the next supply drop would come.

They rationed their supplies carefully, stretching the rice and lentils as far as they could, but it was the tea that became their lifeline.

Every afternoon, when the cold seemed most unbearable and the isolation pressed down on them like a weight, they would gather around the small stove and brew a pot of tea. It was weak, made with tea leaves that had been reused more times than they could count, but it was hot, and it brought with it a sense of routine—something familiar in the midst of the unknown.

As they sipped their tea, they talked. Not about the glacier or the cold or the constant threat of disaster, but about home. They shared stories of their families, of childhood memories, of the meals they missed and the festivals they longed to celebrate. It was a way to remind themselves of who they were, of the lives they had left behind, even if only for a little while.

"I miss my mother's cooking," Iyer said one afternoon, his voice soft as he stared into his cup. "She used to make the best biryani. The smell alone would fill the whole house."

Verma nodded in agreement, a wistful smile on his face. "My grandmother used to make the best parathas. Every Sunday morning, like clockwork."

Arjun, listening quietly, felt a pang of longing for his own home. He hadn't told his parents the truth about where he was stationed, and though they had sent letters, the distance between them felt insurmountable at times. The tea, though weak and lukewarm, reminded him of the small comforts he had taken for granted.

As they sat together, sharing memories and sipping tea, the glacier outside seemed a little less daunting. They were still trapped, still cut off from the world, but in that moment, they had each other—and the warmth of home, if only in their minds.

The Day the Bathroom Flew Away

Morning on the glacier was always unforgiving. As the men stirred in their sleeping bags, cocooned in layers of warmth, they knew the world outside was a frozen wasteland. Getting up was a battle, the cold seemed to have its own weight—pushing against their will to rise, daring them to face the biting winds of the Siachen Glacier. Every morning was the same ritual: a hurried scramble to bundle up in as many layers as possible, then the inevitable trek to the one place no one wanted to go—the bathroom.

The "bathroom," as they called it, was little more than a glorified tin shack. Positioned precariously at the edge of post, it offered the only semblance of privacy in a world otherwise dominated by the open, indifferent expanse of ice. Built from old tin sheets, some worn-out canvas, and scavenged wooden planks, the structure barely held together on the best of days. It wasn't uncommon to hear the metal creak in the night, the wind rattling it like a warning. But no matter how flimsy, it was their only shelter from the elements when nature called.

However, one particular morning, something was amiss. Verma was the first to notice.

"Where the hell's the bathroom?" he yelled, his voice echoing across the camp. He stood, hands on his hips, staring at the spot where the makeshift outhouse had once proudly stood.

Arjun, groggy and still rubbing the sleep from his eyes, stumbled out of the barracks. "What are you talking about?" he mumbled, not yet fully awake.

Verma pointed dramatically toward the vacant patch of snow. "Look. It's gone."

Arjun blinked, his brain still trying to process the situation. He squinted into the bright reflection of sunlight on snow, only to realize Verma was right. The entire bathroom had vanished. All that remained was a small depression in the snow, surrounded by a few scattered tin scraps. The realization hit him like a cold slap to the face—their only refuge from the brutal cold when they needed it most had disappeared, likely swept away by the howling wind.

"What the…" Arjun muttered, approaching the spot cautiously. "Did the wind really take it?"

Sharma, ever the practical one, appeared behind them, surveying the scene with an expression of weary acceptance. "Must've been the storm last night," he said, shaking his head. "The wind probably tore it right out of the ground."

By now, the rest of the camp had gathered, equally bewildered. Iyer, with his usual sarcasm, ran his fingers through his tangled hair and let out a mock gasp. "So let me get this straight—while we were snug in our bags, the wind decided to have a little fun and took our only bathroom on a joyride across the glacier?"

"Seems like it," Arjun replied, still staring at the empty space in disbelief. "I mean, I know the winds are strong here, but I didn't think they'd be strong enough to carry away half our camp."

Iyer shook his head in mock seriousness. "What's next? The mess tent? Should we start tying everything down?"

A few men chuckled, though the humor was thin. The reality of their situation was quickly sinking in. The bathroom wasn't just a convenience—it was a lifeline. Without it, they'd have to face the glacier's biting cold and the indignity of doing their business out in the open, with nothing but the elements to shield them.

Verma groaned loudly, rubbing his gloved hands together. "So what do we do now? Just dig a hole and pray the wind doesn't freeze us solid?"

Sharma crossed his arms and sighed. "Well, unless you want to use the barracks..." he trailed off, his voice laden with dry humor. "Guess we're back to basics."

The loss of the bathroom quickly became the greatest inconvenience the soldiers had faced in a long time. Sure, they'd endured food shortages, storms, frostbite scares, and the constant mental strain of isolation, but this—this was a new level of discomfort.

Morning routines, which were already rushed to minimize time spent in the cold, now became a logistical nightmare. With no bathroom, the men resorted to the most basic solution they could think of: shovels. Every morning, pairs of soldiers would trudge out into the snow, armed with a shovel and a roll of toilet paper, searching for a semi-sheltered spot where they could dig a makeshift latrine.

It wasn't long before they discovered that even the most carefully dug holes couldn't shield them from the cold winds. The glacier's ever-present gusts whipped through the air, stinging their faces, freezing any exposed skin, and making the entire process feel like a cruel joke.

"Man, this is the worst," Verma groaned as he stood in knee-deep snow, clutching a roll of toilet paper. "I can't feel my toes, and I haven't even started yet."

Arjun, standing a few feet away, muttered through chattering teeth, "You're lucky if it's just your toes. My fingers feel like they're about to fall off."

The wind howled around them, whipping snow into their faces, and the cold was relentless. Even layered in multiple pieces of clothing, the biting chill seemed to find its way through every crack and crevice.

"Remember when we used to complain about the bathroom being too cold?" Verma said, his voice barely audible over the wind. "Now I'd kill to have it back. Tin walls and all."

The makeshift latrines were far from perfect. Half the time, they'd dig a hole, only to have it immediately filled back in by the swirling snow. The other half of the time, the wind would kick up just as they were finishing, threatening to blow away the precious roll of toilet paper.

"Hold onto that!" Arjun yelled one morning, watching in horror as a gust caught the edge of the toilet paper Verma had been holding. Verma dove for it, barely catching it before it blew off into the distance.

"Can't even trust the damn wind anymore," Verma muttered, clutching the roll like it was the most valuable thing in the world.

The others had similar stories. Iyer, who always seemed to have a knack for bad luck, had managed to drop his gloves in the snow while fumbling to dig a hole one morning. By the time he'd picked them up, his hands had turned red from the cold, and he'd spent the rest of the day nursing his numb fingers by the heater.

The wind was merciless, the cold unforgiving, and the daily routine of finding a place to relieve themselves became a dreaded task.

After days of suffering through the relentless wind, numbing cold, and the sheer indignity of digging holes in the snow, Major Sharma, known for his practical and sometimes unorthodox thinking, finally had enough. The daily latrine struggle had become the highlight of every conversation, and morale was beginning to suffer. Something had to be done.

Sharma stood at the center of the room, his arms crossed and a look of determination etched on his face. "We need a better solution," he announced, breaking the heavy silence.

"For what?" Verma muttered, rubbing his gloved hands together. "The cold? The wind? The fact that we're living on this cursed glacier?"

Sharma smirked. "For the latrine situation. It's unacceptable."

Arjun, seated nearby with a mug of rapidly cooling tea, raised an eyebrow. "You have a better idea than digging holes and praying the wind doesn't blow us away mid-business?"

"As a matter of fact, I do." Sharma strode over to the corner of the room and pulled out a roll of tarpaulin. He slapped it onto the table with a flourish. "We're going to build something permanent. Something that doesn't involve frostbite or the indignity of squatting in a snowstorm."

The men exchanged skeptical glances. "You're serious?" Iyer asked.

"Dead serious," Sharma replied. "We're going to build a fortress—a Snow Fortress Latrine."

The Construction

Despite their initial skepticism, the men were drawn in by Sharma's enthusiasm. Armed with wooden beams, plywood, metal sheets, and a healthy dose of stubbornness, they began their work.

First came the frame, constructed from sturdy wooden beams scavenged from supply crates. Sharma supervised as Verma and Iyer hammered the pieces together, their movements clumsy in thick gloves.

"Make sure it's solid," Sharma barked over the wind. "I don't want this thing toppling over in a blizzard."

Next, they covered the frame with sheets of metal and plywood, securing them with nails and rope. Arjun, with his medical precision, ensured the seams were tight. "We don't want the wind sneaking through the cracks," he said, his breath misting in the icy air.

The insulation came next. They packed snow against the outside of the walls, forming a thick, windproof barrier. The tarpaulin was stretched over the roof, reinforced with planks and anchored to the ground.

Inside, they installed a wooden seat over a deep, covered pit dug into the snow. Sharma, ever the perfectionist, fashioned a sliding lid to cover the pit when not in use.

"Last touch," Sharma said, holding up a kerosene heater and a roll of reflective foil. The heater was placed in a corner, shielded by a metal box to prevent accidents, and the foil was lined along the walls to amplify both heat and light.

The First Use

The Snow Fortress Latrine was ready by evening, standing proud against the harsh backdrop of the glacier. It was a marvel of ingenuity, a testament to their resilience.

"Who's testing it first?" Sharma asked, his eyes scanning the group.

All eyes turned to Verma.

"Oh, come on," Verma groaned. "Why is it always me?"

"Because you're the bravest," Arjun quipped, grinning.

Grumbling, Verma grabbed a flashlight and trudged outside. The others crowded around the frosted window, watching as he disappeared into the snowstorm. Minutes passed before he reemerged, a triumphant smile on his face.

"It's warm," Verma declared as he stepped inside, shaking off the snow. "And private. I think I might have shed a tear of joy."

The men erupted into cheers, their laughter echoing through the barracks.

Chapter 7

BREAKING POINT

The Glacier's Grip

Every morning, before the rest of the camp stirred, Arjun would bundle himself into his thick winter gear and lace up his heavy boots to come to the edge of the ice wall.

It always reminded him of how vulnerable they were, a handful of souls defying the might of the mountain and the unforgiving cold. But at the edge of that thought lay a stubbornness, a refusal to be beaten by the glacier's isolation and indifference.

The ice wall itself was a natural barrier, a sharp drop-off into a ravine that seemed bottomless. Arjun had made it his habit to come here, not out of recklessness, but as an act of defiance and reflection. This spot, where the world seemed to end, felt like the only place he could fully confront the weight he carried—the responsibility of keeping his men safe, the constant threat of avalanches, and the gnawing worry for those who would never make it home.

He would stand there for minutes that felt like hours, letting the cold numb his body even as it cleared his mind. The wind howled in his ears, a constant companion, and the glacier stretched endlessly below, a harsh and beautiful reminder of nature's power.

Some mornings, Arjun would bring a steaming cup of tea, the heat radiating through the metal mug and into his gloved hands. He'd sip it slowly, the warmth fighting against the chill, and think of home—of family dinners, laughter, and warmth that had nothing to do with temperature. But more often, he just stood there, letting the silence speak volumes.

When the sun rose, casting pale, almost ethereal light across the glacier, Arjun would take a deep breath, savoring the stillness one last time. Then he would turn, his boots leaving fresh tracks in the snow as he made his way back to camp. Each step was deliberate, each movement a calculated effort to conquer both the terrain and the creeping sense of isolation.

By the time he returned, the men would be awake, readying themselves for another day of hard labor and bitter cold. Arjun would greet them with a nod or a word of encouragement, slipping effortlessly into his role as their leader. But for those moments at the edge of the ice wall, he was just a man—a man staring into the vast unknown, fighting battles that no one else could see.

That daily routine became a ritual, an anchor in a world that offered little certainty. It was there, on the edge, that he found a semblance of control and reminded himself of who he was—not just a soldier, but a guardian of hope in a place that seemed determined to strip them all of it.

And so, each day, he would go back to the edge. Back to the wind, the cold, and the silence that somehow felt like home

Major Sharma's Reflections

Inside their shared tent, the weak heater hummed, struggling to fend off the cold that seemed to permeate everything. Arjun collapsed onto his cot, his eyes drifting to the photograph of Zoya that he kept in his jacket. He had looked at it so many times that the edges of the picture had begun to fray, but the image of her smile still brought a warmth that the glacier could never offer.

Sharma, sitting across from him on his own cot, noticed the way Arjun's expression tightened as he gazed at the picture. He didn't need to ask what was on Arjun's mind; he had seen that look before—on countless soldiers who were slowly being worn down by the distance, the cold, and the crushing isolation.

"No letters yet?" Sharma asked gently, though he already knew the answer.

Arjun shook his head, not looking up from the photo. "It's been weeks," he said, his voice quieter than usual.

The silence between them stretched out, heavy and filled with unspoken concerns. It was a silence both men were used to by now—the kind that the glacier imposed on all of them, seeping into their thoughts and gnawing away at the edges of their sanity. Sharma knew how much the distance from home could weigh on a man, especially in a place like this. He had been through it himself, and he could see that Arjun was now facing the same battle that had once tested him.

"You know," Sharma began, his voice softer now, "I had a similar experience when I did my time with the Rashtriya Rifles. It was one of my toughest assignments, but not because of the fighting. It was because of the waiting."

Arjun glanced up at him, surprised. Sharma rarely spoke about his previous postings, and when he did, it was usually to give advice or share a story that had a lesson behind it. But this felt different—more personal.

"I was posted in Kashmir for a while," Sharma continued. "Not my first posting, of course. I'd been through the usual rotations—infantry, counterinsurgency duties in the northeast—but Kashmir was different. There were nights up there where we'd go weeks without any action, just waiting. Waiting in the cold, waiting in the quiet. And the thing is, it's not the bullets that get to you in places like that—it's the silence."

Arjun stayed quiet, listening. Sharma's voice had a certain calmness to it, but there was a weight behind his words that only years of experience could bring. Arjun had always respected Sharma's leadership, but hearing him speak like this—opening up about the things that weighed on him—made Arjun realize how much they had in common.

"We were stationed in a remote area," Sharma said, leaning forward slightly as he spoke. "And it wasn't just the cold that got to us. It was the isolation. The feeling that we were forgotten, stuck up there while the rest of the world moved on. The quiet messes with your head. You start to wonder why you're there. But that's when you learn the most about yourself—when there's no one to fight, no distractions, just you and your thoughts."

Arjun nodded slowly, understanding more than he wanted to admit.

Arjun leaned back on his cot, his eyes still on the photograph of Zoya. "It's hard, though," he admitted. "When the letters stop... when it feels like you're out of sight, out of mind. You start to wonder if they're moving on without you."

Sharma's expression softened. "I know," he said, his voice low. "But you've got to remember why you're here. You're not fighting for yourself. You're fighting for your men. And when you're back home, you'll realize the people who matter never really forgot you. They're just waiting, like you are."

Sharma paused for a moment, his mind drifting to memories of home. "You know, my grandparents came to India during the Partition. They had to leave everything behind, but my grandfather always said, 'As long as you know where you came from, you'll never be lost.' I think about that whenever I'm out here. We might be far from home, but we know where we belong. Don't let this place make you forget that."

Arjun gave a small nod, his grip tightening slightly on the photo. Sharma's words echoed in his mind, offering a bit of clarity in the fog of uncertainty that had settled over him. He knew that Zoya hadn't truly forgotten him, but the silence—the weeks without a letter—had made it feel as though the distance between them was growing larger with each passing day.

Sharma, sensing that Arjun needed some space to process his thoughts, stood up and stretched, rubbing his hands together for warmth. "We all feel it, Arjun," he said, his tone lighter now. "The distance, the cold, the isolation. But the key is to hold on to the things that matter. And trust me—when this is all over, you'll look back on this and realize just how strong you really were."

Arjun watched as Sharma moved toward the small stove to heat some tea. The older officer had a way of cutting through the noise in his mind, offering advice that was simple but profound. As Arjun lay back on his cot, he felt a small flicker of hope—a reminder that he wasn't alone in his struggle, that the men around him were all fighting the same battles, both on the glacier and within themselves.

And somehow, that made the cold a little more bearable.

Republic Day Pizza

The next morning, the usual silence of the camp was broken by a buzz of excitement—an unexpected bit of news had reached them. Word had spread that Domino's Pizza had arranged a special delivery to the glacier for Republic Day. In a place where the men were used to nothing but Maggi noodles, frozen rations, and endless cups of tea to stay warm, the idea of real pizza was almost too good to believe.

By the time breakfast was over, the men were already talking about it with a mix of disbelief and humor. In the mess tent, Verma and Iyer, always the first to start a joke, were already speculating wildly about what the pizza might be like when it finally arrived.

"I don't believe it," Verma said, shaking his head in disbelief as he sat down next to Iyer. "Pizza? Here? How in the world did they manage that?"

Iyer, ever the optimist, grinned as he warmed his hands near the heater. "They are probably frozen" he replied. "By the time it gets here, we'll be eating pizza popsicles."

Verma laughed at the thought, and even Rathod couldn't resist joining in on the banter. He was busy stirring yet another pot of the ever-present Maggi noodles, but the corners of his mouth lifted into a smile as he spoke.

"I'll bet you it's colder than this damn glacier," Rathod said dryly. "And I'll take any bets that it's going to be harder than these noodles."

The others chuckled in agreement. Maggi had been their staple meal for so long that any variation seemed like a distant dream. The idea of something different—anything other than noodles—had the entire camp in good spirits. The promise of pizza, even if it was a ridiculous notion in such a remote place, had lightened the mood, and for the first time in days, the men allowed themselves to feel a spark of excitement.

When the helicopter finally arrived in the late morning, a ripple of energy ran through the camp. The soldiers rushed outside, their breath clouding in the freezing air as they gathered to watch the delivery. The snow whipped around them as the chopper's blades churned, and the sight of the boxes being unloaded from the cargo hold was met with cheers and laughter.

The excitement reached a peak when the pizzas were carried into the mess tent, the cardboard boxes stacked high on the table. The men eagerly gathered around, tearing open the boxes with a childlike anticipation, only to find... exactly what they had feared. The pizzas were frozen solid. The cheese was hard as ice, the crusts brittle from the cold, and the toppings frozen in place like tiny glaciers on each slice.

For a moment, there was silence as the men took in the absurd sight of what was supposed to be their grand feast. Then, Verma broke the silence, holding up a slice of pizza that looked more like a piece of frozen bread than anything remotely edible.

"This is a joke, right?" Verma said, his voice tinged with mock outrage as he waved the frozen slice in front of him. "They must have meant to send us bricks, not pizza!"

Iyer, who had predicted this from the start, burst into uncontrollable laughter. "Pizza popsicles! I called it!" he exclaimed between gasps of laughter, slapping Verma on the back. "I told you, man, frozen pizza is the only pizza we're going to get up here."

Even Rathod, who normally kept his emotions in check, couldn't help but chuckle at the sheer absurdity of the situation. "I knew it would be cold, but this is ridiculous," he said, shaking his head in amusement as he picked up a slice that cracked in half under the slightest pressure.

And then there was Arjun, who had been quieter than usual over the past few days. Even he couldn't help but crack a smile at the sight of his men trying to gnaw through their icy pizzas. The absurdity of the situation—the notion of eating pizza on the world's highest battlefield, only to find it frozen solid—was exactly what they all needed to break the monotony. For a moment, the glacier's oppressive cold and isolation seemed distant, replaced by shared laughter and camaraderie.

Determined not to let the pizza go to waste, the men gathered around the small heaters, trying to thaw the slices enough to take a bite. The process was slow, and the pizza, now partially defrosted, was far from what they had hoped for. The cheese remained rubbery, the crust soggy in some parts and still rock-hard in others, but no one complained. It wasn't about the quality of the food—it was about the sheer novelty of it, the break from routine, and the laughter that filled the mess tent.

Verma, still grinning from ear to ear, raised his half-thawed slice in mock toast. "To the best damn pizza we've ever eaten on a glacier!" he declared, his voice full of humor and irony.

The men laughed and followed suit, raising their frozen slices in unison. "To Republic Day!" Rathod added with a smirk, as he bit into a slice that still crunched slightly from the frost.

They huddled around the heaters, talking and laughing as they worked their way through the strange meal. There was no tension in the air, no anxiety about what the next day would bring—only the warmth of camaraderie that came from shared experience, even if that experience was eating frozen pizza in one of the harshest environments on Earth.

As the laughter continued to fill the mess tent, Arjun leaned back in his chair, his slice of pizza untouched in his hand. For the first time in a long while, he felt the tightness in his chest loosen, even if just for a few minutes. He looked around at his men—Verma, Iyer, Rathod, and the others—and realized how much moments like this mattered. Up here, in the frozen expanse of Siachen, these moments of laughter and absurdity were what kept them going.

It wasn't the pizza itself that had lifted their spirits. It was the fact that, for a few hours, they had something to laugh about. Something that wasn't the cold or the danger or the endless waiting. It was a reminder that, despite everything, they were still human. Still capable of finding joy in the smallest, most ridiculous things.

As the afternoon wore on, the laughter began to die down, and the men returned to their tasks, but the memory of the Republic Day pizza remained. It was a story they would tell for years to come—how Domino's Pizza had made it to the glacier, only to be frozen solid.

Facing the Coldest Winter

The laughter from the Republic Day pizza soon faded as the men settled back into the cold, unyielding reality of life on the glacier. As the sun dipped below the horizon, the temperature plummeted faster than usual, the bitter cold settling in for the night. It was going to be the coldest night in years, perhaps the coldest in over a decade.

Inside the camp, the soldiers braced themselves for what they all knew would be a grueling night. The tents shook with every gust of wind, the sound like a distant rumble of thunder. The weak heater in Arjun and Sharma's shared tent struggled against the encroaching cold, barely able to warm the small space around it. It sputtered now and then, fighting against the elements with everything it had, but both men knew it wasn't enough to fully stave off the chill that had settled into their bones.

Sharma sat hunched over on his cot, pulling his blanket tighter around his shoulders. His breath fogged in the air, visible with every exhale. "This is the coldest winter I've ever seen," he muttered, rubbing his hands together for warmth. His voice was low, the kind of voice that didn't need to rise above a whisper to be heard clearly in the tense quiet of the tent.

Arjun sat across from him, his eyes fixed on the flickering flame of the heater, as if willing it to grow stronger. The harsh, flickering light cast deep shadows on his face, accentuating the exhaustion etched into his features. He had been through a lot in the last few months—physically, mentally, emotionally—and the cold only made it worse. The glacier, in all its unforgiving nature, seemed determined to break them. "How much longer do you think we can hold out in this?" Arjun asked quietly, his voice barely audible over the wind outside.

Sharma glanced at him, his expression calm, though his eyes betrayed a deep weariness. He had been through more winters in harsh conditions than he cared to remember, but this one felt different. But, like always, Sharma's voice remained steady. "As long as we need to," he said, pulling his blanket tighter. "It's not about the cold—it's about endurance. We just keep going. That's all there is to it."

Arjun nodded, though his mind remained uneasy. He knew Sharma was right—endurance was the only thing keeping them alive at this point. But tonight, the cold felt more personal, more oppressive, like it was testing them in ways they weren't sure they could handle. The wind outside picked up, rattling the tent walls as though the glacier itself was trying to claw its way in.

The night dragged on, the temperature continuing to drop, and soon even the hardiest among them could feel the strain. In the tents, the men huddled together for warmth, their breath visible in the freezing air, their bodies wrapped in every layer of clothing they could manage. Blankets, jackets, even sleeping bags—nothing seemed to stop the bone-chilling cold from creeping in.

Javed, who had been showing signs of improvement in the past few days, now seemed to be slipping again. His usual easy demeanor had been replaced by a nervous restlessness. His eyes, which had begun to regain some light after his earlier breakdown, now looked distant once more, clouded by the weight of the cold and isolation. He sat quietly in the corner of the mess tent, his arms wrapped tightly around himself, shivering despite the layers of clothing he wore.

Arjun watched him carefully, the concern evident in his eyes. He could see it happening—the glacier was getting to Javed again, like it had before, eroding his will and his sense of self. And if it could get to Javed, who had been so close to breaking before, it could get to any of them. "Javed, you alright?" Arjun asked gently, trying to keep his voice steady, even though the concern was clear.

Javed didn't respond right away, his eyes focused on the floor as though he hadn't heard the question. After a long pause, he looked up, his face pale and his voice barely more than a whisper. "It's too quiet," he said, his words barely audible above the wind. "Too quiet... too cold. I don't know how much longer I can do this."

Arjun felt a pang of worry deep in his chest. He had seen that look before in other men—men who had reached their breaking point, who had stared into the abyss for too long. He leaned forward, his voice soft but firm. "We're all feeling it, Javed. But we're going to get through this. One day at a time. Don't let this place get into your head."

Sharma glanced at Javed from across the tent, his eyes narrowed in concern. "He's right, Javed. The cold... it messes with your head. But you're stronger than that. We've made it this far together, and we'll keep going together."

Javed nodded weakly, though the look in his eyes remained uncertain. The cold was relentless, and the isolation was taking its toll on all of them.

A Moment of Humanity

One afternoon, during a routine patrol, Arjun led his team across the glacier, their figures barely visible through the swirling snow. The wind was fierce, whipping at their faces, and visibility was low. The patrol was a routine one, meant to ensure that the camp's perimeter remained secure. As they trudged through the deep snow, their breaths heavy and labored in the thin air, something caught Arjun's eye.

Across the ridge, just visible through the haze of blowing snow, there was movement—figures moving in the distance. Pakistani soldiers.

For a brief moment, everyone froze. The presence of the enemy so close to their position brought with it an immediate sense of tension. The soldiers gripped their rifles a little tighter, their eyes narrowing against the wind as they watched the figures across the ridge. Both sides were separated by an expanse of snow and ice, but even that distance felt insignificant in the vast emptiness of the glacier.

Arjun's mind raced as he assessed the situation. It wasn't the first time they had spotted Pakistani troops from their patrol routes, but it was always a tense moment. The ceasefire between the two countries was delicate at best, and up here, misunderstandings could easily escalate into something far more dangerous. He signaled to his men to hold position, their hands poised and ready.

For what felt like an eternity, both groups stood still, watching each other across the frozen expanse. The wind howled between them, and the only sound was the crunch of ice under their boots as they adjusted their stances. The tension in the air was thick, every man acutely aware of the rifles slung over their shoulders and the years of history that divided them.

But then, something unexpected happened.

One of the Pakistani soldiers, a figure barely distinguishable in the snowstorm, lifted his arm and waved. It was a simple gesture, one that could easily have been misinterpreted, but the intent behind it was clear. It wasn't an act of hostility. It was an act of humanity.

Arjun hesitated for a moment, unsure of how to respond. The weight of his responsibility as an officer pressed on him—any action he took could have consequences. But there was something disarming about the gesture, something that felt deeply human. Slowly, he raised his hand and waved back.

The rest of the soldiers on both sides remained still, watching the brief exchange in silence. The wind howled around them, the snow falling in relentless sheets, but for that moment, the tension eased. It was a small, almost insignificant act, but it held a power that none of them could have predicted.

Arjun lowered his hand, and the Pakistani soldier did the same. The two groups continued to watch each other for a few moments longer before the patrol resumed its course. The soldiers across the ridge slowly disappeared back into the whiteout, just shadows now, swallowed by the storm.

As they trudged forward through the snow, the moment stuck with Arjun. It was a fleeting gesture, a brief connection in the midst of this frozen, hostile environment, but it spoke volumes. Up here, on the world's highest battlefield, they were all fighting the same battle, not against each other, but against the glacier itself. The real enemy wasn't the men standing on the other side of the ridge—it was the cold, the isolation, the sheer relentlessness of this place.

Arjun's thoughts lingered on the soldier who had waved. He wondered what that man was thinking, if he, too, had been feeling the weight of the glacier pressing down on him, wearing him thin. In the end, they were all just men trying to survive in one of the harshest places on earth. The politics, the borders, the uniforms—none of it mattered when you were standing on a glacier, fighting for your life against the elements.

As the patrol continued, Arjun glanced at his men. Verma and Iyer were trudging through the snow just ahead, their faces hidden behind scarves and goggles, their movements slow and deliberate as they fought against the biting wind. Rathod, ever vigilant, was scanning the horizon for any signs of movement. And behind them, Javed marched in silence, his breath visible in the freezing air. They were all tired, worn down by the endless cold, but they kept moving forward. They had to. There was no other option.

That night, as they gathered around the weak heater in the mess tent, the moment still weighed on Arjun's mind.

Sharma noticed the distant look in Arjun's eyes as they sat together, huddled around the small heater. "Something on your mind?" he asked, his voice low so as not to disturb the others, who were busy trying to thaw their hands and feet.

Arjun glanced at him, then shook his head, a faint smile tugging at the corner of his mouth. "Just thinking about the patrol today."

Sharma raised an eyebrow, sensing there was more to it. "Anything interesting happen?"

Arjun hesitated for a moment, then said, "We saw some Pakistani soldiers on the ridge. One of them waved at us."

Sharma's expression softened slightly, and he nodded. "It happens sometimes. Out here, the enemy isn't always who you think it is."

Arjun nodded in agreement. "It's the glacier, isn't it? The cold, the isolation... it gets to all of us. Doesn't matter what side of the border you're on."

Sharma leaned back slightly, his eyes reflecting the flickering light of the heater. "Exactly. Up here, we're all just trying to survive. It's easy to forget that sometimes. But moments like that... they remind you."

Arjun didn't say anything more, but he felt the weight of Sharma's words settle into his mind.

Chapter 8

THE GLACIER'S FURY CONTINUES

The wind howled relentlessly, as if the glacier was determined to break them. Each day, the men seemed to grow quieter, their movements slower. What little energy they had left was spent trying to keep warm and stay alive. The sky, perpetually gray, offered no comfort, and the cold felt as though it was seeping into their bones.

Arjun could feel his body deteriorating further. Each morning, as he tried to rise from his cot, his joints ached from the constant exposure to the cold. His muscles, once strong and defined, had withered away. The 12 kilograms he had lost since arriving on the glacier was a constant reminder that the glacier was slowly but surely claiming them all, piece by piece.

He looked around at the men. Their eyes were hollow, their cheeks sunken, their uniforms darkened with soot from the kerosene heaters that seemed to offer little warmth but plenty of grime. They had grown gaunt, their faces marked by the harsh reality of survival.

Each conversation felt heavier now, the jokes rarer, the laughter almost extinct.

The Company Commander's Resolve

Major Sharma had always been a rock—a stoic leader the men could look up to. Arjun admired how Sharma managed to stay calm under pressure, always composed even as the glacier slowly chipped away at everyone.

It was late afternoon, and the temperature had dropped once again, making even the short walk from their tents to the mess hall feel like an ordeal. Arjun walked into their shared tent, finding Sharma sitting quietly at the edge of his cot, staring down at a small photo he held in his hand.

Arjun didn't need to ask what the picture was—he knew it well. It was of Sharma's wife and daughter, the baby girl born just a year ago. The major had spoken fondly of her several times since they had been posted on the glacier, always with a smile that momentarily brightened his otherwise serious expression.

"The big day is tomorrow, isn't it?" Arjun asked gently, sitting down across from him.

Sharma nodded, his face hard to read, but there was a sadness behind his eyes. "Her first birthday."

Arjun leaned forward, feeling the weight of the moment. A child's first birthday was a milestone—a celebration of life, family, and love. And Sharma, sitting here thousands of feet above sea level, surrounded by snow and ice, was missing it.

"I wish I could be there," Sharma said quietly, his voice steady but tinged with regret. "I've missed so much already. Her first steps, her first words… and now this."

Arjun didn't speak right away, knowing that nothing he could say would lessen the ache Sharma felt. "She'll understand when she's older," he offered after a moment. "She'll know why you couldn't be there."

Sharma looked up at Arjun, a firm resolve behind his faint smile. "I know she will," he said, his voice steady, filled with quiet confidence. He glanced back at the photograph, his expression softening. "You don't need to explain why we're here. We've all sworn an oath. It's not about the glacier, the cold, or even the distance. It's about the duty we chose."

Arjun nodded, recognizing the steel behind Sharma's words. It wasn't that Sharma didn't feel the weight of his family's absence; it was that he had made peace with it long ago. For men like Sharma, the call to serve was never about convenience or timing. It was about something greater, something that transcended personal moments, no matter how significant.

"Being here, on this frozen battleground," Sharma continued, his voice unwavering, "it's all part of it. The hard part isn't being away from them—it's making sure we're strong enough to go back when it's time. That's what I focus on. Every day, every step, is another one closer to that."

Sharma took a deep breath, slipping the photograph carefully back into his jacket. "Tomorrow is her first birthday," he said, his voice steady, though there was a hint of something softer beneath. "I won't be there to hold her, but I'll imagine it. I'll picture her laughing, probably trying to grab the cake with both hands. She's a little warrior in her own way."

Arjun smiled, the image vivid in his mind. He could see it—Sharma's daughter, tiny but full of energy, reaching out with determination. Though thousands of kilometers separated them, Sharma's pride was unmistakable.

"You'll be there soon enough, sir," Arjun said, trying to offer reassurance. "And when you are, she'll know exactly who her father is—one hell of a man."

Sharma chuckled softly, the sound warm but brief. "Maybe," he said. "But even if she doesn't understand everything now, I know the day will come when she'll realize why I'm here. Why we're all here. It's the duty we've chosen, Arjun, and there's no room for second-guessing. Our families… they're stronger than we think. They carry us just as much as we carry them."

Arjun admired the major's resolve. Sharma had always been a man of few words when it came to personal matters, but when he spoke, there was a conviction that left no room for doubt. Despite the heartache, despite missing such a significant moment in his daughter's life, Sharma never wavered in his dedication.

"You're right," Arjun said thoughtfully. "It's not just about being here. It's about why we're here. And when we go back, it'll all make sense."

Sharma gave him a small nod, his eyes distant for a moment as though lost in thought. Then he straightened, pushing the cold and the distance aside with a determined expression. "We have to keep reminding ourselves of that," he said firmly. "Every single day. Because out here, if you lose sight of it, you lose yourself."

The two men sat in silence for a moment, the weight of Sharma's words settling over them like the cold outside the tent. But there was a strength in that silence—a shared understanding that, no matter how far away their families were, the bond they held with them was unbreakable.

"You're not just a good father," Arjun said after a while, breaking the quiet. "You're a damn good leader too. We see it every day."

Sharma's faint smile returned, one of quiet acknowledgment. "Thanks, Arjun. But out here, it's all the same. Being a father, being a leader—it's about taking care of your people, even when you're not with them."

As the light outside the tent faded into the long night, Sharma glanced towards the tent flap where the icy wind threatened to break through. "We hold the line, no matter what," he repeated, almost to himself. "For them. For all of us."

"We may be far away," Sharma said quietly, his eyes reflecting the fading light outside, "but we're never truly apart."

Arjun's Growing Anxiety

That night, Arjun lay in his cot, once again struggling to breathe. His body felt heavy, his chest tight as if an invisible weight was pressing down on him, squeezing the air from his lungs. He tried to shift, propping himself up with extra pillows, but the relief was minimal.

The hypoxia had worsened. Every night, it was the same—he'd wake up gasping for breath, his heart racing, panic surging through him. In those moments, the walls of the tent seemed to close in, the suffocating cold wrapping around him a vice.

He had told no one about these episodes. How could he? The men were already looking to him to hold things together. If they knew their captain was struggling, it would only add to their own fears. But with each passing night, Arjun wondered how much longer he could endure it.

The attacks weren't limited to the night anymore. During the day, he often found himself short of breath, especially after the smallest exertion—carrying supplies, walking across the camp, even getting dressed in the morning. His body was breaking down, and there was nothing he could do about it.

Senior To Junior

One night, as the wind outside howled like a beast clawing at the walls of the camp, Arjun and a few others gathered around the small heater inside the tent. It was in moments like these, when the temperature seemed to sink the lowest and the silence pressed in the hardest, that Arjun often thought back to the stories his mentor, Colonel Bhardwaj, had told him. There was one story in particular that had always stayed with him—one from Bhardwaj's younger days, during the Kargil War, when he wasn't yet the battle-hardened officer Arjun had come to respect, but a young army doctor thrust into the chaos of war.

Bhardwaj had shared the story one evening after a long day of training, back when Arjun was still a cadet. They were sitting under the shade of a tree, their uniforms dusty and their bodies exhausted. The Colonel, normally so composed and stern, had a rare moment of openness, talking about the time when he was much younger and untested, much like Arjun was then.

"I wasn't always a hardened officer, you know," Bhardwaj had said, a faint smile on his lips. "Back in the day, I was a young doctor—a captain at the time—posted to a forward area in the north during the Kargil conflict. I had never seen combat before, not like that."

The Kargil War was one of the most intense and brutal battles in recent Indian military history, and even though Arjun had studied it extensively, hearing Bhardwaj's personal account was different. There was a gravity to the Colonel's words that couldn't be found in textbooks.

"We had set up a makeshift field hospital not far from the frontlines," Bhardwaj had continued, his voice taking on a more serious tone. "The shells were falling day and night, the sound of gunfire was constant, and we were getting wounded soldiers almost every hour. Some of them… well, let's just say, no amount of medical training prepares you for the kind of injuries I saw. It was hell."

He had paused then, as if the memories were still too vivid. Arjun remembered the look in his eyes—distant, but also resolute, the mark of a man who had seen the worst and survived.

"There was one night I'll never forget," Bhardwaj had said after a moment. "We were in the middle of a massive artillery barrage. The Pakistanis were shelling our positions relentlessly. The field hospital was getting hit with debris, and the ground was shaking so hard, I thought the roof was going to come down on us. But we couldn't stop. The wounded kept coming in, and we were all that stood between them and death."

Bhardwaj had taken a deep breath, his fingers flexing slightly, as if they still remembered the feel of blood and bandages. "There was this young soldier, no older than you are now, Arjun. He had taken a piece of shrapnel to the abdomen—severe internal bleeding. When they brought him in, I didn't think he would make it. But something about the look in his eyes… he wasn't ready to die. He was fighting, even with all that pain. And I knew I had to fight for him too."

The Colonel had gone quiet for a moment, and Arjun had held his breath, waiting for him to continue.

"I worked on him for hours," Bhardwaj had said, his voice quieter now. "Through the shelling, through the chaos, we kept going. The lights went out at one point, and we had to use torches to see what we were doing. But we didn't stop. I didn't stop."

Arjun had felt a shiver run down his spine, not from the cold, but from the weight of Bhardwaj's words. The Colonel was describing a moment where life and death hung in the balance, and where a young doctor had been thrust into a role far beyond what he had ever expected.

"In the end, we saved him," Bhardwaj had said, his lips curling into a faint smile. "He made it. I don't know how, but he pulled through. And that's when I realized something important about being a soldier—about being a doctor in the army. It's not just about following orders or sticking to protocol. Sometimes, it's about pushing yourself beyond what you think you're capable of, because lives are depending on you. You don't have the luxury of fear or hesitation."

The Colonel had looked at Arjun then, his gaze sharp, piercing. "That was my first real battle—not with bullets or enemies, but with time, with death, with the overwhelming urge to give up. And I'll tell you something, Arjun: that's a battle you'll face out here too. On this glacier. It's not the cold or the enemy that will break you—it's the voice inside your head telling you to quit. That's the real fight."

Arjun had never forgotten those words. Now, as he sat on the glacier, the biting wind outside their tent reminding him of how fragile life could be in this frozen wasteland, he thought of Bhardwaj and the lessons he had passed on. The Colonel had fought his battle in the heat of Kargil, under the constant threat of death, but the lesson was the same. It was about resilience, about digging deep and finding the strength to keep going, even when every part of you wanted to stop.

A Sudden Tragedy: A Jawan's Fall

It had started as a routine task, something the men did nearly every day—retrieving supplies from the newly established trolley system that ran along the ice wall. The system had been set up to bring much-needed provisions across the glacier, saving the men the arduous and dangerous journey they once had to make on foot.

The men worked quickly, eager to finish the job and get back to the relative warmth of their tents. Arjun was overseeing the operation, watching as the trolley creaked its way along the cable, loaded with crates of food, kerosene, and medical supplies.

Ritin Kumar was part of the team hauling the supplies in from the trolley. He was young, strong, and always quick with a grin, even in the harshest conditions. Today, however, there was a tension in the air that Arjun couldn't quite place.

"Kumar, watch your footing," Arjun called out as the young soldier leaned over the edge of the ice wall, trying to reach one of the crates that had swung out of position on the trolley. The ice beneath his boots was slick, and Arjun could see it glisten dangerously under the weak sunlight.

Kumar gave a quick nod, his gloved hand gripping the edge of the trolley's platform as he reached further out to pull the crate back. For a moment, everything seemed fine— just another routine maneuver.

And then, without warning, a deep crack echoed through the air.

Arjun's heart leaped into his throat. The ice wall beneath Kumar gave way with a sudden, sickening lurch, crumbling like brittle glass. Arjun watched in horror as Kumar lost his footing, his arms flailing for balance as the icy ground beneath him disappeared.

"Kumar!" Arjun shouted, his voice drowned out by the howling wind and the terrifying sound of ice shattering all around them.

In a blink, Kumar was gone, swallowed by the glacier as the ice wall gave way entirely. The world seemed to slow down as Arjun ran toward the edge, his boots skidding on the ice. He reached the lip of the crevasse just in time to see Kumar's body tumbling down the jagged slope, crashing into the ice below with a sickening thud.

For a moment, everything was still. The wind howled, but the men were silent, staring in shock at the place where Kumar had stood just moments before.

"Get ropes!" Arjun barked, snapping out of his daze. "Now! We need to get down there!"

The men scrambled into action, grabbing ropes and gear from the supply tent as quickly as they could. Verma stood frozen at the edge, still staring down in shock.

"Verma!" Arjun's voice was firm, cutting through the fog of fear. "Get it together. Help secure the ropes."

Verma blinked, snapping out of his daze, and nodded, moving quickly to assist the others. Arjun didn't wait for the gear to be ready. He grabbed his medical kit, slinging it over his back, and began securing a harness around his waist.

The ice wall was steep—too steep for a clean descent—but there was no time to think about the danger. Arjun's mind was already on Kumar, calculating the chances of survival. From this height, the fall had to have been catastrophic. But there was still a chance, a slim hope maybe Kumar was still alive, clinging to life somewhere beneath the snow and ice.

When the ropes were finally secured, Arjun moved to the edge, testing the tension with a few sharp tugs. The rope felt sturdy enough, but the conditions made everything more dangerous. The wind howled viciously, whipping across the ice wall, and the surface below looked slick and uneven, the jagged outcroppings of ice offering little to no foothold.

"Lower me slowly," Arjun called up to the men, his voice steady despite the storm raging in his mind.

The descent began, the rope sliding through Arjun's gloved hands as he carefully navigate his way down the wall. Each step was deliberate, his boots finding purchase on small ridges of ice, but the surface was treacherous. The cold had frozen every surface to a glassy sheen, and Arjun could feel his boots slipping. His heart pounded in his chest as the wind howled around him, buffeting his body and threatening to throw him off balance.

One slip, one misstep, and he could follow Kumar into the abyss.

As he lowered himself further, the world around him seemed to shrink. The camp above became a distant memory, and all that existed was the ice wall in front of him and the small figure of Kumar growing closer below. Arjun's breath came in short, sharp bursts, the strain of controlling the descent combined with the thin air and cold making every movement feel a monumental effort.

"Steady," he muttered to himself, his voice barely audible over the wind. "One step at a time."

His gloved hands gripped the rope tightly, and every few meters, he paused to check his footing, glancing down at Kumar's unmoving form. The jagged ice below reflected the weak sunlight, blinding him at times, forcing him to stop and squint before continuing. Sweat formed beneath his helmet, a mix of fear and exertion, but the freezing wind quickly turned it to ice against his skin.

Halfway down, the rope jerked unexpectedly, causing Arjun's foot to slip on a patch of slick ice. His heart leapt into his throat as he struggled to regain his footing, his boot scraping against the ice as he fought to steady himself.

"Hold the line!" he shouted up, his voice hoarse with tension.

The men above reacted immediately, holding the rope firm, and after a moment, Arjun managed to stabilize himself. His breath came in ragged gasps now, the close call reminding him how precarious his position was.

Another few feet. He was almost there.

As he neared the bottom, the full extent of Kumar's injuries became painfully clear. His body was contorted, his limbs bent at unnatural angles, his uniform torn and streaked with blood. Arjun swallowed hard, forcing down the rising nausea.

When his boots finally touched the snow at the bottom of the ice wall, Arjun exhaled sharply, relieved to be on solid ground, though the sight of Kumar lying motionless in front of him brought a new wave of dread. He unclipped himself from the rope and hurried over to the fallen soldier, kneeling beside him in the snow.

"Kumar," Arjun said softly, even though he knew the chance of a response was slim.

He reached for Kumar's wrist, searching for a pulse. His fingers pressed against the cold skin, but there was nothing. No flicker of life. His skin was icy, his body unnaturally still.

Arjun's breath hitched in his throat. He checked again, moving to Kumar's neck, pressing his fingers against the artery. Still nothing.

"Damn it," Arjun whispered, the realization hitting him a blow to the chest.

For a moment, Arjun knelt there, his hands still on Kumar's body. The glacier had claimed another life. He knew, logically, this place was dangerous—men died in conditions like this. But knowing it and witnessing it were two different things. Kumar had been one of the youngest in the unit, full of energy, always quick with a joke to lighten the mood. And now he was gone, his life snuffed out in an instant by one misstep.

Arjun's mind raced, his training pushing him forward even though he knew, deep down, it was too late. He opened his medical kit, pulling out the basic tools of his trade, and began performing CPR, his hands moving on autopilot.

"One… two… three…" he counted, pressing against Kumar's chest, his movements precise, methodical, and desperate.

He continued for several minutes, his breath growing ragged as he tried to bring Kumar back. But the truth was already clear—Kumar was gone, his body too broken, the fall too great.

Arjun sat back on his heels, his hands trembling in the cold, the weight of the situation crashing over him an avalanche. The glacier had taken another one, and there was nothing he could do to stop it.

The men above were shouting down to him, asking if Kumar was still alive, but Arjun couldn't bring himself to respond right away. His body felt heavy, his breath shallow as he stared at Kumar's lifeless form.

Finally, after what felt like an eternity, he stood, his legs stiff and unsteady. He turned to the rope and signaled to the men above.

"He's gone," Arjun called, his voice hoarse with grief. "Lower the stretcher."

The wind carried his words up to the men, and soon after, they began lowering a stretcher down to him. Arjun watched as the ropes carried it slowly over the edge, his mind numb as he prepared to carry out his grim task.

When the stretcher reached him, he worked quickly, lifting Kumar's body with as much care as he could manage. The jagged edges of the ice had torn at Kumar's clothes, and Arjun could see the extent of his injuries—broken bones, deep lacerations. It was a miracle he had survived the initial impact at all, even if only for a few moments.

As Arjun secured Kumar's body onto the stretcher, the weight of the loss hit him fully. The cold, the isolation, the constant fear—it had taken its toll on all of them. But Kumar's death was a reminder of how fragile they were out here. One wrong move, one mistake, and it was over.

Once the stretcher was secured, Arjun clipped himself back into the harness and gave the signal to be pulled up. The ascent was slow, each tug of the rope dragging him and Kumar's body back up the ice wall. The weight of the stretcher made the climb more difficult, and every inch felt like a battle against gravity and the glacier itself.

The wind was relentless as Arjun ascended, each pull of the rope accompanied by the sharp sting of icy air against his face. The wind was relentless, whipping through the crevasse with such force it felt as if the glacier itself was trying to resist his efforts, trying to pull him and Kumar's body back into its icy grip. His breath came in ragged bursts, each exhale a visible puff of vapor in the freezing air, and his hands gripped the rope so tightly he could feel his knuckles aching under his gloves.

The ascent was slow, agonizingly slow. The weight of the stretcher beneath him made each step a struggle, and the jagged ice that had threatened him on the way down was now an even greater hazard. His boots scraped against the frozen surface as he carefully maneuvered his way upward, the rope straining under the combined weight of his own body and the lifeless form of Kumar.

Every few feet, he had to stop and check his grip, making sure the stretcher didn't snag on any sharp outcroppings of ice. His arms burned with exertion, his muscles already weakened from months on the glacier, but he forced himself to keep going. Failure wasn't an option. Not now.

Above him, the men worked in silence, pulling the ropes with steady determination. Arjun could hear their labored breaths, the occasional grunt of effort as they hauled him up inch by inch. The tension in the air was palpable, the weight of Kumar's death hanging over them all.

Arjun's thoughts raced as he ascended. He couldn't help but think of how easily it could have been him—one misstep, one moment of distraction, and he too could have fallen. The glacier had a way of reminding them how precarious their existence was, how fragile life could be in a place like this.

As he neared the top, his foot slipped on a particularly slick patch of ice, sending his body lurching sideways. The rope jerked violently, and for a heart-stopping moment, Arjun thought he might lose his grip entirely.

"Hold tight!" he shouted, his voice barely audible over the wind as he scrambled to regain his footing. His hands clung desperately to the rope, his heart hammering in his chest.

The men above responded quickly, tightening the rope and holding it steady as Arjun found his balance once more. He took a deep breath, steadying himself before continuing the final few feet of the climb.

When he finally reached the top, Verma and Rathod were there, their faces drawn with tension. They extended their hands, helping Arjun and the stretcher over the lip of the ice wall and back onto solid ground. The moment his feet hit the packed snow, Arjun felt a rush of relief, though it was quickly tempered by the grim reality.

Kumar's body lay on the stretcher between them, his uniform torn and bloodied, his face pale in the cold light of the glacier. The men gathered around in a somber silence, their expressions grim as they looked down at the fallen soldier. No one spoke. The wind was the only sound, howling mournfully through the camp as if the glacier itself was lamenting the loss.

Arjun unhooked himself from the harness, his hands trembling slightly from both the cold and the emotional toll of the last hour. His body ached, his muscles protesting the strain of the climb, but the pain was nothing compared to the weight in his chest—the crushing sense of helplessness came with knowing Kumar was gone and there had been nothing he could do to save him.

"We'll need to prepare him for transport," Major Sharma said quietly, his voice hoarse. His eyes were fixed on the ground, unable to meet Arjun's gaze.

Arjun nodded, though he felt numb. The world around him seemed to blur for a moment, the cold biting at his skin, but his mind was elsewhere—lost in the memories of Kumar, of the young soldier's laugh, his energy, his spirit. And now, it is gone. Snuffed out by the glacier's unrelenting cruelty.

Together, they lifted the stretcher and carried it back to the center of the camp, where the rest of the men stood waiting in silence. The atmosphere was heavy, the weight of Kumar's death pressing down on everyone. Even the usual chatter and murmurs had died away, replaced by a thick, oppressive stillness.

As they reached the medical tent, Arjun set the stretcher down gently, his hands lingering for a moment on the edge. He felt a knot tightening in his throat, but he swallowed it down, forcing himself to remain composed. The men were looking to him for strength, for guidance, and he couldn't let them see the cracks were starting to form inside him.

The words felt hollow, but it was the only thing he could offer them—the only semblance of control in a situation had spiraled out of their hands. The men nodded solemnly, though no one spoke. The glacier had taken so much from them already, and Kumar's death was another reminder of how fragile their existence truly was out here.

Arjun stood for a moment longer, staring down at Kumar's still form, before turning away. The tightness in his chest had returned, the familiar pressure building as he struggled to catch his breath. He knew what was coming— the panic, the breathlessness—but he couldn't afford to break down. Not now. Not in front of the men.

He walked quickly away from the gathering, heading toward the far edge of the camp where the wind howled the loudest. The cold bit into his skin, but he welcomed it, letting the icy air wash over him as he stood alone, his back to the camp. His breath came in shallow gasps, each one a battle against the tightness gripped his lungs.

With a deep, shuddering breath, Arjun opened his eyes and turned back toward the camp. The men were still standing in silence around the medical tent, their heads bowed in mourning for Kumar. There was nothing more to say. Nothing could ease the pain of the loss.

As he reached the medical tent, he saw everyone standing with their faces lined with exhaustion and grief.

After a few moments, Rathod finally spoke, his voice low and filled with weariness. "This place… it's killing us, one by one."

Arjun turned to look at Rathod, seeing the exhaustion etched into his features. He wasn't wrong. The glacier had taken its toll on all of them. Physically, mentally, emotionally. And now, with Kumar's death, it felt the glacier was slowly tightening its grip around their throats.

"We'll make it through," Arjun said, though the words felt hollow even as he spoke them. "We have to."

Rathod didn't respond. He stared into the distance, his eyes glazed over, as if he couldn't bear to focus on the present anymore. Iyer turned to go, heading toward the tent to help with preparations for Kumar's eventual transport. The rest of the men, still gathered nearby, had started to disperse, retreating to their own tents to process the loss in their own way.

Arjun remained where he stood, staring at the spot where Kumar's body had been carried. The overwhelming weight of responsibility pressed down on him harder than ever. It wasn't about keeping the men alive anymore. It was about holding them together, keeping them sane, preventing the glacier from taking more than it already had.

But the truth was, Arjun wasn't sure how much longer he could keep it up.

The Men's Fraying Morale

In the days following Kumar's death, the camp grew even quieter, the weight of the tragedy hanging over everyone a cloud. Conversations were brief, and the men kept to themselves more than usual, the isolation settling deeper into their bones. Even the routines that had once provided some sense of normalcy now felt a burden.

Arjun noticed it in the way the men moved—slower, with less purpose. The way they spoke—short, clipped words, as if every sentence was an effort. The glacier had taken more than their strength; it had begun to sap their will, their ability to hope.

Rathod, usually the one to keep spirits high with his jokes and light-hearted banter, had grown quiet. Arjun watched him from across the mess tent, noting the way Rathod sat hunched over his food, barely touching it. His eyes were distant, unfocused.

The other men followed suit, each retreating into themselves as the days passed. The wind howled through the camp, a constant reminder of the glacier's unyielding presence. And with each gust of icy air, Arjun could feel the morale of the camp slipping further and further away.

One evening, as they gathered in the mess tent for their meager dinner, Rathod finally spoke up, his voice cutting through the heavy silence.

"How much longer do you think we'll last out here?" he asked, not looking up from his plate.

The question hung in the air, uncomfortably direct. The men glanced at each other, but no one responded right away. Arjun felt his stomach tighten. It was the question that had been on everyone's mind, but no one had dared to ask it out loud.

Arjun set his fork down, clearing his throat. "We'll last as long as we need to," he said, trying to sound confident, though he wasn't sure if he believed it himself.

Rathod let out a bitter laugh, shaking his head. "We've already lost Kumar. And how many more? How long until the next one of us falls off the damn ice wall or gets buried under an avalanche? This place... it's cursed."

Iyer shifted uncomfortably, looking down at his plate. The other men remained silent, but Arjun could see the fear in their eyes. They were all thinking the same thing.

"This place is testing us, Rathod," Arjun said, his voice steady but firm. "And we're stronger than it is."

Rathod finally looked up, his eyes dark with exhaustion and frustration. "Are we? Because it doesn't feel like it."

The mess tent fell silent again, the only sound was the howling wind outside. Arjun didn't have an answer to. He wanted to reassure them, to tell them they would get through this, but the truth was, he didn't know how much longer they could last either. The glacier was relentless, and everyday felt a new test of their endurance.

But they had to survive. They had to.

Arjun's Struggles With His Own Health

In the days following Kumar's death, Arjun's own health began to deteriorate even further. The hypoxia that had been plaguing him for weeks grew worse, making it harder to breathe, even during the day. Every movement felt like a struggle, and even the smallest exertion left him gasping for air.

At night, the attacks were worse. He would wake in the darkness, his chest tight, his lungs burning as he fought to pull in enough oxygen. The sensation was terrifying—drowning on dry land. His heart would race, panic flooding his body as he sat up, propping himself up on two or three pillows in a desperate attempt to make breathing easier.

But no matter how many pillows he used, no matter how he adjusted his body, the relief was minimal. The attacks would last for minutes, sometimes hours, before finally subsiding, leaving him drained and trembling in the cold.

The lack of sleep was wearing him down, both physically and mentally. His mind felt foggy, his thoughts scattered. He knew he couldn't let the men see how much he was struggling, but hiding it was becoming harder with each passing day.

One afternoon, while inspecting the camp's supplies, Arjun bent down to pick up a small crate, and immediately felt a wave of dizziness wash over him. His vision blurred, and for a moment, he thought he might pass out. He straightened up quickly, clutching the edge of the crate to steady himself as his breath came in shallow, ragged gasps.

Verma, who was standing nearby, noticed the sudden change in Arjun's demeanor. He rushed over, concern etched on his face.

"Sir, are you alright?"

Arjun forced a smile, nodding weakly. "I'm fine. Just… a little lightheaded."

Verma didn't look convinced. His eyes scanned Arjun's face, taking in the dark circles under his eyes, the pallor of his skin.

"Sir, with all due respect, you don't look fine," Banerjee said quietly. "You've been pushing yourself too hard."

Arjun shook his head, trying to brush off the concern. "I'm tired, Verma. We're all tired."

But Verma didn't back down. "Sir, you're the one holding this place together. If you don't take care of yourself…"

Arjun exhaled sharply, feeling the weight of Verma's words settle over him. He knew Verma was right, but admitting he was struggling felt like admitting defeat. And if the men saw him faltering, what would do to their already fragile morale?

"I'll be fine," Arjun said, his voice firmer this time. "We're almost through this."

Verma didn't push the issue any further, but the look in his eyes told Arjun he wasn't convinced.

As Verma walked away, Arjun remained standing by the crate, his mind a chaotic swirl of exhaustion and doubt. His body was betraying him, and he knew it. Each day, the effort to maintain control, to keep leading, was becoming more taxing. He was supposed to be the one holding everything together, yet the cracks in his own resilience were growing wider. His breath still hadn't fully steadied, and he placed a hand on his chest, feeling his heart race beneath his fingers.

The thin air was relentless, and the glacier seemed to be winning.

After a moment, Arjun shook his head and continued with his work, forcing himself to ignore the dizziness clung to him.

A Glimmer of Hope

Arjun was going through his usual routine—checking supplies, making notes of the conditions—when Major Sharma approached him, his expression unreadable. He held a small piece of paper in his hand, but it was the look in his eyes that caught Arjun's attention.

Without a word, Sharma handed him the paper. Arjun unfolded it slowly, his fingers stiff from the cold, and as he read the brief message, time seemed to stop. Relief washed over him, though he kept his composure, staring at the words for a long moment, barely able to believe what he was seeing.

Relief Team Dispatch Confirmed.

"We're going home," Sharma said quietly, breaking the silence.

Arjun looked up at him, the weight of the glacier that had pressed down on them for months suddenly feeling a little lighter. He could see the same emotions flickering in Sharma's eyes—relief, disbelief, maybe even a hint of pride. They had made it. Despite everything, despite the relentless cold, the isolation, the loss of Kumar—they had survived.

"Thank you, sir," Arjun finally said, his voice hoarse, though he wasn't sure if he was thanking Sharma for delivering the message or for his constant steadiness throughout their ordeal.

Sharma placed a hand on Arjun's shoulder, his grip firm but warm. He smiled faintly, his face lined with exhaustion but his posture still as solid as ever. "We did it together."

By the afternoon, Arjun had called the men together in the mess tent. The tension in the air was palpable as they gathered, their faces drawn with fatigue but their eyes filled with curiosity. When Arjun stood before them, he took a deep breath, steadying himself. This moment was one he had imagined a thousand times in the darkest hours of the night, but now that it was here, the words came slowly.

"Men," Arjun began, his voice firm but low, "we're going home."

For a moment, there was silence. The words seemed to hang in the air, almost too heavy to comprehend. Then, slowly, the realization began to sink in. The glacier hadn't broken them. They had survived.

Rathod was the first to react, leaning back in his chair and letting out a long, slow breath, the weight visibly lifting from his shoulders. "We made it," he said quietly, a smile tugging at the corner of his mouth.

Verma, who had been staring at his hands, looked up in disbelief, his face breaking into a grin. "We're actually leaving this place?" he asked, his voice barely above a whisper.

Arjun nodded, his own emotions finally starting to surface.

The murmurs spread quickly through the room, the disbelief giving way to a cautious kind of hope. Some of the men exchanged glances, others leaned back in their chairs as if the news had physically knocked the wind out of them. The glacier, this frozen nightmare they had been trapped in for so long, would soon be nothing more than a memory.

Arjun scanned the room, his gaze finally landing on Major Sharma, who was sitting quietly at the end of the table. Sharma gave him a small nod, his expression calm, though Arjun knew how much this moment meant to him. They had all been tested, in ways they never could have imagined, and now, at last, the end was in sight.

"You've all been through more than anyone could ask," Arjun continued, his voice growing stronger. "But you did it. You made it through the worst this place could throw at us. And now, we're going home."

The men's reactions were subdued, but the atmosphere in the room had shifted. There was a sense of lightness now, a feeling had been missing for so long. For months, they had fought against the glacier, against the cold, against their own fears and doubts. And now, they had won.

As the meeting ended and the men began to drift back to their duties, Arjun remained at the front of the room for a moment longer, watching them. He felt a deep sense of pride—not just in himself, but in his men, in the way they had held together through the darkest days..

Hope.

Chapter 9

LEAVING THE GLACIER

The Relievers' Struggles

The first sign of the relief team's arrival came through binoculars—dark, shadowy figures moving cautiously across the glacier. Arjun stood at the edge of the camp, the cold biting into his face as he watched them approach. The path leading up to their forward post was treacherous—a winding route that demanded skill, caution, and, above all, respect for the glacier's unforgiving terrain.

"They're moving too slow," Rathod muttered beside him. His gaunt face, once full of humor, was now etched with fatigue and the silent wariness that came from months of enduring the glacier. "They're going to be in trouble soon."

Arjun handed the binoculars to Iyer, who squinted through them. "One of them slipped," he murmured grimly.

Arjun took the binoculars back and zeroed in on the struggling group of soldiers. One of them dangled precariously from a collapsed ladder, his boots kicking above the gaping maw of a deep crevasse. His comrades were scrambling to pull him up, their movements frantic, the danger clear. The glacier, as always, was waiting to claim another life.

"They need help," Arjun said sharply. "Let's go."

Gathering a small team, Arjun, Rathod, and Verma quickly geared up and began their descent. The path was icy and treacherous, even for those who had spent months on the glacier. For the fresh men of the relief team, it was proving to be a brutal initiation.

As they reached the struggling group, Arjun saw that the soldier suspended over the crevasse had been safely pulled up, though he was clearly shaken. But the relief soldiers' troubles didn't end there. One of their men, a young soldier, was slumped against an ice ledge, coughing violently, his breath coming in short, ragged gasps.

"Pulmonary edema," the new medical officer, Dr. Rawat, said, his voice tight with anxiety as Arjun knelt beside him. "He's got fluid building in his lungs. He's not responding to oxygen."

The diagnosis hit Arjun hard. Pulmonary edema was one of the deadliest conditions at these altitudes, where the thin air made even breathing a struggle. If untreated, it could be fatal within hours. The dark clouds gathering in the sky were a grim reminder that they were running out of time.

"How soon can we get a helicopter?" Dr. Rawat asked, his voice edged with desperation.

Arjun glanced up at the roiling sky. The wind had already picked up, and the air was growing colder by the minute. "Not in this weather," he said firmly. "We'll have to keep him here and stabilize him."

Dr. Rawat's face drained of color. "I—I don't know if we can."

"We don't have a choice," Arjun replied, his tone decisive. He could see the fear in the young doctor's eyes—the glacier was testing him too, just as it tested every man who set foot on it. But there was no time for hesitation. The soldier's life hung in the balance.

The HAPO Bag Saves the Day

The group worked swiftly, the cold biting into their fingers as they retrieved the HAPO bag from their emergency supplies.

The High-Altitude Pulmonary Oxygenation bag was a life-saving device for cases exactly like this—when there was no time or means to descend and evacuation was impossible.

Arjun helped position the struggling soldier inside the bright orange, inflatable chamber, securing it as Dr. Rawat adjusted the oxygen levels and sealed the bag.

"Is he going to be okay?" Verma asked, his breath fogging in the freezing air, his eyes filled with concern.

"We'll find out," Arjun replied, his voice calm but tense.

As the bag began to inflate, the pressure inside simulating the lower altitudes where the oxygen concentration was higher, Arjun and the men waited in silence. The soldier inside the bag coughed weakly, his breathing still labored, but slowly, it began to stabilize. The bag was doing its job—forcing more oxygen into his lungs, giving him the vital air he needed to survive.

"It's working," Dr. Rawat whispered, relief flickering across his face as he monitored the soldier's vitals. His initial fear had been replaced by a quiet determination, the confidence that came from seeing his actions yield results.

Arjun stood back, watching as the soldier's breathing eased, the color slowly returning to his pale cheeks. They had bought him time, but Arjun knew the real test was ahead. The storm was coming, and they still needed to wait for the right moment to evacuate him safely.

"Keep him in there as long as he needs," Arjun told Dr. Rawat. "We'll get him down as soon as the weather clears. For now, focus on keeping him stable."

Dr. Rawat nodded, still shaken but more composed now. "Yes, sir. I'll stay with him."

Arjun stepped back, exchanging a look with Rathod. The danger had passed for now, but the weight of their situation was ever-present. The glacier had spared them today, but they all knew how quickly things could change. One misstep, one unexpected storm, and the glacier would claim another life.

The Handover Procedure

The storm had finally passed, but the air was still thick with tension as the handover began. Arjun and Major Sharma stood at the center of the camp, reviewing the final details of the rotation with Major Yogesh Rao, the incoming company commander.

Dr. Rawat was still monitoring the soldier in the HAPO bag, ensuring that his recovery was steady.

Arjun walked over to Dr. Rawat, placing a hand on his shoulder as they both stood near the makeshift medical tent where the patient was resting inside the HAPO bag.

"Dr. Rawat," Arjun began, his voice steady, "this isn't like treating soldiers back in the base hospital. It's relentless out here. You did well today, but remember—it's not just the cold you'll have to fight. It's everything. Exhaustion, fear, isolation. You'll see it in the men and feel it in yourself."

Rawat looked up at Arjun, his youthful face shadowed by uncertainty. "I didn't expect it to be this hard. I thought I was prepared, but out here... it's different."

Arjun nodded slowly, his expression serious. "No one's really prepared for this place. But you have to keep going. The men will look to you. You're their lifeline."

Sharma, ever the calm and experienced leader, looked over the supply lists and personnel files with Rao, his tone firm and authoritative. "You'll need to keep a close watch on your men in the coming weeks," Sharma advised. "The glacier doesn't care if they're fresh—it will test them like it's tested us. Keep an eye on their health, and don't let anyone push themselves too far."

Major Rao listened intently, nodding in agreement. "Understood, sir. We're ready for it."

As the final signatures were exchanged, Sharma handed over the command with a sense of quiet satisfaction. His time on the glacier was coming to an end, but the weight of responsibility would now shift to Major Rao. He extended his hand to the new company commander, giving him a firm grip, a gesture filled with the silent understanding of what lay ahead.

The wind howled outside the command tent, a constant reminder of the unforgiving environment they had been battling for months. In the distance, the rhythmic thumping of helicopter blades began to echo across the camp, signaling the arrival of the airlift team. The storm had subsided just enough for a chopper to make the treacherous flight up to their altitude.

The helicopter landed with a heavy thud on the icy surface, snow swirling around as its blades chopped through the frigid air. Arjun turned to look at the patient being readied for evacuation. The soldier, who had battled pulmonary edema and narrowly survived thanks to the HAPO bag, was now being gently loaded onto the stretcher and carried toward the waiting chopper. Dr. Rawat, who had tended to him with dedication, walked alongside, ensuring everything was in place for the flight.

Arjun watched as the helicopter disappeared into the distance, feeling a sense of closure—both for the evacuated soldier and for his own time on the glacier. It wasn't just the end of their mission; it was the end of a chapter that had tested them all in ways they could never have imagined.

As the snow settled back down, Major Sharma turned to Major Rao and spoke with the quiet authority that had guided them through countless challenges. "You'll find your rhythm here," he said, his tone steady. "The glacier's going to test you, and your men, every single day. But remember, it's about survival. Endurance. Don't let it break you."

Rao nodded, understanding the weight of the words. "We'll hold our ground."

With that, the handover was complete. The old guard—Arjun, Sharma, and their team—prepared for their departure, gathering their gear and taking one last look around the camp that had been their home for so long. They were leaving behind the glacier, but the men replacing them would now face the same cold, the same isolation, the same unforgiving environment.

As Arjun turned to leave, he paused for a moment, looking back at Rao and his men. "Good luck," he said quietly, though the words held a depth that went beyond their simple meaning. He knew how much Rao would need it.

For Major Rao and his men, the real battle was just beginning.

The Descent Journey: A Final Trial

Major Sharma stood beside Arjun, his eyes scanning the horizon. Behind them, Major Rao's men had already started to settle into the camp, their presence a silent reminder that the cycle would continue.

Arjun addressed his team one last time before they set off. "This isn't over until we're off the glacier. Stick together. Keep focused. The terrain will be treacherous, and the weather's unpredictable."

Sharma, standing nearby, gave a firm nod. "We've come this far. We're not losing anyone on the way down."

With that, they began their descent

The men set off from their post, just as the faintest light began to pierce through the heavy blanket of winter clouds. Each step felt deliberate, as though the glacier itself had been waiting for their departure, and the landscape, once familiar from their arrival, had transformed into something foreign and dangerous. Sharma led the group, his senses alert as he scanned the path ahead, while Arjun kept an eye on their rear, measuring the progress of every man.

Their journey had begun with hope. Relief was on the horizon—base camp and safety just days away. But the glacier was not so easily conquered. The months of isolation, extreme cold, and physical strain had taken their toll on everyone. Every soldier had grown weaker, their bodies hardened to the ice but drained of vitality. The reality was far more taxing than any of them had imagined when they first arrived.

The descent from the glacier was supposed to be a relief, but it quickly proved to be a final test, one just as brutal as the months they had spent at the top.

As they moved forward, the terrain quickly revealed itself to be nothing like what it had been when they had first ascended. The narrow ridges had become treacherously slick, and the snowpack had shifted into unstable drifts that obscured the path beneath. What once had been relatively solid ground now felt like walking on shifting sand. Where they had initially climbed with strength and determination, they now moved with caution and fatigue.

The men trudged forward, their boots sinking into the fresh powder, each step more difficult than the last. It wasn't long before they encountered their first major obstacle: a wide crevasse that hadn't been there during their ascent. The group came to a halt, staring at the deep crack in the ice, the bottom of which was shrouded in darkness. Arjun's eyes swept across the men, noting the exhaustion on their faces, but there was no turning back now.

"We need to rope up," Arjun said, his voice firm, though fatigue was clearly etched into his features. "We'll move across in pairs. No one goes alone."

Sharma stepped forward to help set up the safety lines, his hands moving methodically despite the biting cold. His breath fogged the air as he spoke quietly to Arjun, "The terrain's shifting fast. This isn't the same glacier we climbed."

Arjun nodded, glancing over the crevasse. He knew Sharma was right. Everything had changed in their absence, and it was going to take all their strength to navigate through the dangers ahead.

One by one, the men crossed the crevasse, their ropes taut as they carefully placed their feet on the fragile ice bridges. Every movement was deliberate, calculated—one wrong step could spell disaster. When it was Arjun's turn, his legs trembled slightly, not from fear but from the sheer exhaustion that had taken root in his muscles after months on the glacier. As he crossed, he felt the ice creak beneath his boots, a stark reminder of just how precarious their journey had become.

Once everyone was safely on the other side, the men shared a collective breath of relief. But that moment was short-lived. The weather was turning, the wind picking up, sending flurries of ice crystals swirling around them like a storm of tiny blades.

"We need to keep moving," Sharma urged, his voice barely audible over the wind.

The Weight of Exhaustion

The physical toll of the journey was beginning to wear on the men, their once-quick pace reduced to a slow, labored crawl.

Arjun could see it in their faces—the dark circles under their eyes, the way their movements had become sluggish and mechanical. They had all grown thin, their bodies wasting away as the glacier drained them of energy. Even Rathod, always the quiet pillar of strength, had slowed, his breath coming in ragged gasps as they moved deeper into the harsh landscape.

Verma, one of the oldest in the group, stumbled more than once, his legs buckling under him as the terrain grew steeper. Arjun moved beside him, placing a steadying hand on his shoulder.

"Take it slow," Arjun said quietly. "We'll get there."

Verma nodded, though his eyes betrayed the fear that had settled into his bones.

The descent stretched into hours, and the group spoke less and less as they moved through the shifting terrain.

Arjun couldn't help but think back to their induction months earlier. They had arrived on the glacier full of energy, determination, and maybe even a bit of excitement. The terrain had been just as unforgiving, but they had tackled it with strength and vigor. Now, the glacier seemed like a different beast entirely. It was as if it had grown more hostile in their absence, reshaping itself into an even more dangerous opponent.

The nights during the descent were the worst. The men huddled together in their tents, trying to stave off the cold with their dwindling energy reserves. Sleep came in brief, fitful bursts, each of them waking to the sound of the wind screaming through the valleys.

The second day of their descent brought even more challenges. The weather had worsened overnight, and by morning, visibility had been reduced to nearly zero.

"Watch your step," Sharma called out, his voice muffled by the wind. "The ice is unstable."

The men moved in a tight formation, each one following closely behind the other as they navigated the narrow ridges and sharp drops. At one point, Verma nearly slipped again, his boot skidding on a patch of ice. Arjun grabbed him by the arm, pulling him back before he could fall.

"Careful," Arjun warned. "We're almost through this stretch."

But they weren't through yet. As they continued, the terrain became even more unpredictable. The snowdrifts had shifted, creating hidden crevices that threatened to swallow them whole. At one point, Iyer stumbled into one of the drifts, sinking waist-deep into the snow. The others rushed to pull him out, their hands moving quickly despite the cold that had numbed their fingers.

"We need to keep moving," Sharma said, his voice firm. "We can't afford to stop now."

The glacier had become a maze of hidden dangers, and the men knew that every step could be their last if they weren't careful. But there was no turning back. The only way was forward, and they had to rely on each other to make it through.

The Final Push

By the third day, the men were running on fumes. Their food supplies were almost gone, and the cold had seeped so deeply into their bones that it felt like they would never be warm again. Every step was a struggle, their bodies protesting with each movement. But they were close now—base camp was just ahead, though it still felt miles away.

Arjun's legs burned with exhaustion, but he forced himself to keep moving. He had to. They all had to.

Sharma walked beside him, his face pale but determined. "Almost there," he said, though it sounded more like a reminder to himself than anyone else.

As they rounded a final bend, the terrain leveled out, and in the distance, they saw it—base camp, nestled at the foot of the glacier like a beacon of hope. The sight of it sent a wave of relief through the group, though they were too tired to express it. Their journey was nearly over, but the weight of the glacier still pressed down on them.

They had made it. Barely. But they had made it.

As they approached the camp, Arjun glanced back at the glacier, the towering walls of ice and snow that had been their prison for so long. It looked as menacing as ever, but now, there was a sense of distance between them and the glacier. They had survived its trials, and soon, they would be free.

When they finally reached base camp, it was as if the weight of the world lifted from their shoulders. The sight of the camp, with its warm shelters and bustling activity, was almost surreal after months of nothing but snow and ice.

Arjun felt a wave of relief wash over him as they were greeted by fresh-faced soldiers, their uniforms crisp and clean compared to the tattered, soiled gear of his own team. The contrast between the two groups was stark—Arjun and his men were gaunt, weathered, their faces darkened by the sun and wind, while the new soldiers looked bright and eager.

As soon as they arrived, Arjun headed to the bathroom, desperate to wash off the grime and see his own reflection for the first time in months. When he looked into the mirror, he barely recognized the man staring back at him. His beard was thick and unruly, his skin dark and rough, with deep lines etched into his face from the relentless cold and wind.

Slowly, he began to shave, each stroke of the razor revealing more of the man he used to be. But even as the beard disappeared, the weight of the glacier remained. The man in the mirror wasn't the same person who had arrived here months ago.

Returning to his quarters, Arjun felt the pull of exhaustion weighing him down. But before he could collapse into his cot, he knew he needed something more immediate: a hot bath.

He stripped off his clothes, layer by layer, the familiar cold fabric sticking to his skin. His hands were cracked and raw, his body leaner and harder from the months of brutal conditions.

When he stepped into the steaming shower, the hot water hit his skin a revelation. For a moment, he simply stood there, letting the warmth pour over him, washing away the layers of grime, soot, and the deep chill had settled into his bones. The steam swirled around him, and he closed his eyes, feeling the tension in his muscles begin to release.

The hot water felt almost too good, after months of nothing but cold. He scrubbed at his skin, watching as the water turned gray, the residue of the glacier being washed away. But as he stood there, he realized something unsettling—the physical grime might be gone, but the mental weight was still there. The glacier had seeped into him in ways no amount of hot water could erase.

The Commanding Officer's Welcome

After cleaning up, Arjun was greeted by Colonel Ghosh, the commanding officer at base camp. Ghosh welcomed Arjun and his team back with a firm handshake and a look of admiration.

"You've done something remarkable, Captain," Colonel said, his voice filled with respect. "Surviving up there, leading your men through it—that's no small feat. Not everyone can handle the glacier."

Arjun nodded, but the praise felt distant. He was proud of what they had accomplished, but the cost weighed heavily on him. The faces of the men they had lost. His pride was tinged with guilt and sadness. He forced a smile for Colonel Ghosh, but it didn't reach his eyes.

"Thank you, sir," Arjun replied. His voice felt distant, almost someone else was speaking for him. He'd made it through the glacier, but a part of him felt he hadn't fully returned yet.

Colonel Ghosh clapped him on the shoulder. "Your team will be debriefed, and then you can rest. We've got real food waiting for you."

The mention of it stirred something in Arjun. The idea of warmth, of comfort, was almost too much to process. It seemed another world—one he was about to step back into, though it felt a lifetime since he had been a part of it.

Later in the day, Colonel Verma called for a brief ceremony to honor Arjun and his men for their service. It was a simple affair, a gathering in one of the mess halls where a handful of officers stood waiting to present them with Siachen Medals—a small token of recognition for the months they had endured at the highest and harshest battlefield on Earth.

Arjun stood at attention with his team, their backs straight, their faces solemn. The men lined up next to him had been through hell. Rathod's eyes had lost their usual spark, Iyer's face looked permanently lined with exhaustion, and even the youngest members of the team carried an air of quiet, haunted resilience.

One by one, they were called forward to receive their medals. Arjun watched as each of his men accepted theirs, their fingers closing around the cool metal as they pinned the medals to their chests. After Sharma's name was called, Arjun's name followed. He stepped forward with steady, deliberate steps.

Colonel Ghosh pinned the medal onto Arjun's chest and shook his hand. "You've earned this, Captain. And I don't say it lightly."

Arjun felt the weight of the medal pressed against his chest. It was a small thing, but it felt heavy—heavy with the memories of the glacier, the lives lost, and the sacrifices made. As he stepped back into line, he felt a mix of pride and sorrow. They had survived the glacier, but they hadn't left it unscathed.

After the ceremony, Arjun needed some air. He stepped outside, leaving the warmth of the mess hall behind, and took a deep breath of the cold, sharp air. But this time, the air didn't have the same bite it did on the glacier. It was cold, but it wasn't the soul-freezing chill he had grown used to.

For the first time in months, Arjun was wearing normal shoes—not the heavy glacier boots that had weighed him down with every step. He looked down at his feet as he walked, feeling the lightness in his steps. It was strange, almost foreign, to move so easily, without the weight of the ice and snow holding him back.

As he walked down the paved roads of base camp, the sensation of solid ground beneath his feet was almost unsettling. The roads were smooth, predictable, unlike the treacherous paths of the glacier where any step could be your last.

The familiar sounds of base camp surrounded him— vehicles rumbling, soldiers talking and laughing, the distant hum of machinery. It was all so normal, yet it felt so distant from the world Arjun had known for the past months. The normalcy of it all felt like a dream.

He passed by groups of fresh-faced soldiers, their uniforms crisp and clean. They glanced at him as he walked by, but quickly returned to their conversations. For them, life was still normal. For Arjun, normal felt something he'd forgotten.

The Food Experience

Arjun joined his team in the mess hall, where real food awaited them. The spread wasn't fancy—rice, dal, vegetables, and roti—but to Arjun and his men, it might as well have been a feast.

Arjun took his seat and served himself a plate. As soon as the food touched his lips, the warm, rich flavors flooded his senses. He hadn't tasted anything like this in months. The rations on the glacier were bland and barely edible, designed for survival, not pleasure. But this meal—it tasted home, comfort.

He ate slowly, savoring each bite, feeling the warmth of the food spread through his body. Around him, the men were doing the same, eating in quiet contemplation. They had survived on so little for so long this meal felt a gift, a reminder they were still alive, still human.

But even as the food warmed him, Arjun couldn't shake the feeling of distance. The food might have been real, but the glacier still clung to his mind. He had made it back to base camp, but he wasn't sure if he could ever fully return to the life he had left behind.

After the meal, Arjun returned to his quarters and pulled out his mobile phone, a device that had been useless on the glacier. It felt strange in his hands, an artifact from a world he barely remembered. When he powered it on, the screen lit up, and the phone buzzed with a flood of notifications—missed calls, messages, emails—all things had been waiting for him in the real world.

The early ones were full of encouragement, checking in, and wishing him well. But as the months passed, the messages became fewer, and their tone more uncertain. People weren't sure when—or if—he would respond.

And then there were the messages from Zoya.

Arjun's heart clenched as he opened the messages. Zoya had been his anchor, the person he thought of during the long, cold nights on the glacier. Her early messages were filled with love and concern, asking how he was, if he was safe, and telling him how much she missed him. But as time went on, her messages became less frequent, shorter. The last one, sent weeks ago, was a single line: *"I don't know if I can keep waiting."*

Arjun stared at the screen, the words blurring before his eyes. He had been so focused on surviving the glacier he hadn't realized how much time had passed, how much had changed while he was gone. The glacier had taken so much from him, and now it seemed it had taken Zoya as well.

The Emotional Weight of Return

As Arjun sat on the edge of his cot, the phone in his hand, he felt the weight of everything pressing down on him. The glacier, the men they had lost, the isolation, the cold—it was all still with him, even though he was back at base camp. The warmth of the food, the shower, the normal shoes—none of it could erase the months he had spent fighting the glacier.

He thought about Kumar, about the men who had slipped away into the glacier's unforgiving grasp, and about those who had barely made it through. Their faces flashed before his eyes, each one a reminder of the toll this experience had taken on them all. He wondered if the warmth of the base camp would ever be enough to thaw out the frost that had taken root in his soul.

Arjun stood up from the cot and set the phone down. The screen still glowed with missed calls, but he couldn't bring himself to answer them. Not yet. Not when the distance between him and the world he left behind felt so insurmountable. Instead, he walked to the small window at the far end of the room, looking out at the bustle of base camp.

The normalcy of it all felt an illusion. He watched soldiers move between the tents, the occasional sound of laughter or idle chatter breaking the monotony of the camp's steady hum. A part of him wanted to join them, to lose himself in the familiarity of routine and comradeship. But he knew no amount of small talk or mundane tasks could erase what he had seen, what he had been through.

As he stood there, staring out into the horizon, a soft knock came at the door.

"Come in," Arjun called, his voice quiet, almost detached.

The door opened, and Rathod stepped in, his face still pale from exhaustion, but his expression soft. There was a bond between the men now that didn't need to be spoken of—a quiet understanding they had survived something extraordinary together.

"Sir," Rathod started, "you all right?"

Arjun gave a small, almost imperceptible nod. "As all right as I can be."

Rathod hesitated for a moment, then stepped further into the room, closing the door behind him. "The men were talking," he continued, his voice low. "About how strange it all feels. To be here. To be… normal again."

Arjun turned away from the window and met Rathod`s gaze. "It's going to take time," he said simply, but there was a heaviness in his tone. "Normal isn't something we can walk back into."

Rathod nodded, understanding. "Troops were asking if you'd join us later. For a drink." He smiled slightly. "We figured we could use a little celebration."

Arjun considered the offer, part of him yearning for the company of his men, the other part wary of pretending everything was okay. But he knew they needed this—some semblance of closure, some small way of marking their return to a world felt far too different from the one they had left.

"I'll be there," Arjun said finally.

Rathod smiled wider this time, relief in his eyes. "Good. I think it'll help."

Rathod left the room, closing the door softly behind him. Arjun turned back to the window, his reflection ghosted in the glass. He stared at his own face for a long moment, the clean-shaven skin still unfamiliar, the lines etched deeper than before.

The Emotional Release

Later in the night, Arjun joined his men in the small, dimly lit mess hall where they had gathered. The atmosphere was subdued but warm, with the familiar clink of glasses and the low murmur of voices filling the space. Rathod, Iyer, and the others sat around a table, their faces softer, more relaxed than Arjun had seen in months.

As he took his seat, a glass was pushed toward him, and Rathod raised his in a small toast. "For making it through," he said, his voice carrying the weight of what those words truly meant.

The men echoed the toast, clinking their glasses together, but the silence followed was thick with everything left unsaid. There were no loud celebrations, no grand speeches.

Arjun sipped his drink, the warmth of the alcohol spreading through him, loosening the knots that had formed in his chest. The conversation around the table drifted from topic to topic, mostly mundane, sometimes drifting into memories of the past. But no one mentioned Kumar, or the close calls, or the long nights spent wondering if they'd ever see the base camp again. It was too soon for it.

As the evening wore on, Arjun found himself watching the men around him. Verma laughed at something Rathod said, his smile genuine for the first time in what felt forever. Rathod, for his part, looked lighter, a weight had been lifted off his shoulders. Even the younger soldiers, who had struggled the most, seemed to have found some peace in the simple act of being together, safe, and warm.

Arjun's heart ached with a strange mixture of relief and sorrow. They had survived, yes—but surviving came with its own price.

Final Farewell at Base Camp

Arjun stood beside a Gypsy, looking out over the camp, the engine idling softly in the background. He would be heading to Leh, where he would catch a flight to Srinagar, finally leaving behind the relentless cold that had defined his existence for months. For the first time in what felt like an eternity, he could sense the weight of the glacier lifting from his shoulders.

Major Sharma approached him, moving with the same deliberate, measured steps that had become so familiar during their time on the glacier. They both knew this was their final conversation before parting ways.

"Well, this is it," Sharma said, stopping just a few feet away. His breath hung in the frigid air, but his voice carried warmth and relief. "We finally made it."

Arjun nodded, a mix of exhaustion and quiet satisfaction etched on his face. "Feels strange, doesn't it? Like we've been up there for years."

Sharma smiled, his eyes reflecting a deep weariness that only those who had shared the glacier's burdens could understand. "Time moves differently up there. Every day feels like a year, and now that we're down here, it's like none of it was real."

They both stood in silence for a moment, the noise of the camp fading away. Arjun's gaze wandered back to the mountains in the distance, the glacier now hidden from view but still looming large in his mind.

"I'll be heading to Leh for a flight to Srinagar in the morning," Arjun said quietly, breaking the silence. "After everything we've been through, it feels unreal to be going back."

Sharma gave a thoughtful nod. "Srinagar will feel like paradise compared to what we've endured. Warm beds, real food… and no ice underfoot at every step."

Arjun chuckled softly, but there was a bittersweet edge to the thought of leaving the glacier behind. "Hard to believe it's all over."

Sharma turned to him, his expression serious but proud. "You did well, Arjun. Surviving that place, keeping the men together… That's no small feat. You're a better leader than you give yourself credit for."

Arjun looked down for a moment, humbled by the words, before meeting Sharma's eyes. "I couldn't have done it without you, sir. You were the anchor for all of us."

Sharma shook his head slightly, his tone firm yet full of respect. "No, Arjun. The men followed you because you gave them something to believe in. You'll carry that with you, wherever you go next."

The silence between them was charged with the unspoken bond they had formed—two soldiers who had not just survived together but had endured and grown alongside one another.

"I guess this is goodbye, then," Arjun said, offering his hand.

Sharma clasped his hand tightly, his grip strong and resolute. "It's not goodbye, Arjun. You'll find your way. And if you ever need to talk, you know where to find me."

Arjun nodded, feeling the weight of Sharma's words settle deep within him. The unspoken support between them had carried them through the hardest days. "Take care, Sir."

With one last nod, Sharma turned and walked back toward the officers' quarters, his silhouette blending into the backdrop of the bustling base camp. Arjun watched him go, feeling a mixture of closure and sadness, knowing their time on the glacier had forged an unbreakable bond.

As Arjun turned to climb into the Gypsy, ready to make his way to Leh, he paused and looked back one final time at the base camp. The life they had known up there—the ice, the cold, the never-ending battle—was behind him now. The glacier had tested him in ways he could never have imagined, but it hadn't broken him. He had survived.

And now, as the engine of the Gypsy roared to life, he was heading home.

Chapter 10

HOMECOMING

The Arrival at Srinagar Airport

Arjun hadn't realized just how much he had changed until the plane began its descent into Srinagar. As the aircraft dipped beneath the clouds, the familiar snow-capped peaks of the Pir Panjal range came into view. The lush green valley stretched out below, dotted with tiny homes and winding roads. It was everything he had yearned for during the long, frigid nights on the glacier. Yet, as the wheels touched the tarmac, the sense of relief he had expected didn't wash over him. Instead, a dull ache of uncertainty settled in his chest.

The airport was bustling with activity—crowds of people, luggage carts wheeled by harried porters, families waiting for loved ones. The noise was overwhelming. After months on the glacier, where silence had been the only constant, the chaotic energy of the city felt foreign. He felt out of place, as if he were moving through a dream, watching the world rush around him but not being part of it.

As he exited the terminal, his friends were waiting, their faces lighting up as soon as they spotted him. Shashank was the first to break through the crowd, his broad smile unmistakable. He rushed forward, wrapping Arjun in a bear hug that knocked the breath out of him.

"Arjun! It's so damn good to see you, man!" Shashank exclaimed, stepping back but still gripping Arjun's shoulders as if to reassure himself his friend was really there.

"You made it!" Raghav added, joining them with a grin that mirrored Shashank's. "You look… thinner. What did they feed you up there? Ice?"

Arjun chuckled, but the sound felt hollow. "Yeah, something like that."

The jokes continued as they grabbed his bags and guided him toward the car, but Arjun found himself drifting in and out of the conversation. His friends' voices seemed distant, their laughter a sharp contrast to the quiet that still lingered in his mind. The glacier had stripped him of noise, of human connection, and now it felt like everything around him was moving too fast, too loud.

"You okay?" Shashank asked, his tone softening as they reached the car.

Arjun nodded. "Just tired. It's been a long journey."

They didn't push any further, sensing something was off. The drive to his house was filled with more light-hearted banter, but Arjun's responses were few and far between. His thoughts were elsewhere—still caught between the present and the glacier, where time had seemed to freeze along with everything else.

The Café Farewell

The café was warm, a stark contrast to the biting cold Arjun had lived in for months. The clatter of cups and low hum of conversation filled the air, but Arjun felt disconnected, as if all the noise was happening somewhere far away. He sat across from Zoya, his hands wrapped around a steaming cup of coffee, but the warmth didn't reach him.

Zoya, sitting opposite him, looked different— more distant than he remembered. She stirred her tea absentmindedly, her eyes darting from him to the window, where the streets of Srinagar buzzed with life.

It had been weeks since he'd returned from the glacier, but this was their first proper meeting. For so long, he had imagined this moment, picturing her running into his arms with tears of relief. But now, as they sat together, the distance between them felt vast.

Zoya broke the silence first, her voice soft but steady. "You look... different."

Arjun smiled faintly, but it didn't reach his eyes. "I feel different."

She gave a small nod, her fingers tightening around her cup. "I can see that."

For a moment, neither of them spoke. Arjun watched her carefully, noticing the way her hands trembled slightly as she held the cup. There was something heavy in the air between them, something unsaid but unavoidable.

"Zoya," he began, his voice tentative, "I know it's been hard. Me being away, everything..."

"It's not just that, Arjun," she interrupted gently, her eyes meeting his, filled with something he hadn't seen before—resignation. "I know why you had to go. I understood it then, and I understand it now. But it's more than just the glacier. It's... it's you."

Arjun's heart sank. "Me?"

Zoya nodded, placing her cup down on the table. She took a deep breath, as if bracing herself for what she was about to say. "You've always needed something more. Always searching for the next adventure, the next challenge. Even before Siachen, you were chasing something—whether it was a mission, a goal, some need to prove yourself. I've stood by you through all of that, but..."

Her voice faltered for a moment, her eyes glistening with unshed tears. "But I'm realizing that I can't keep waiting. I can't keep holding on to something that's never still."

Arjun felt a wave of confusion and panic rise in his chest. "I'm not leaving again, Zoya. I'm here now. I thought that's what mattered."

Zoya's smile was sad, as if she'd heard those words before. "But it's not just about being here physically, Arjun. It's about what drives you. You've always been looking for something else—something bigger than us. And I understand that, I really do. But I can't be the one waiting anymore. I need stability. I need someone who chooses *us*, not the next mission."

Arjun blinked, feeling the weight of her words settle heavily on his shoulders. He had always thought Zoya understood why he did what he did—why the need to prove himself was so important. He had never considered that it might push her away.

"I thought you understood," he whispered, his voice strained. "This is who I am. I love you, Zoya, but I also love what I do. It's not about choosing one over the other... it's just... I need both."

Zoya shook her head gently, her fingers nervously playing with the edge of the napkin in front of her. "I know you do. And that's why I can't stay, Arjun. You've always been chasing something out there, and I don't think you'll ever stop. I've tried to be okay with it, but I need something different. I need someone who wants a quieter life. Someone who isn't always looking for the next mountain to climb."

Her words felt like a punch to the gut. Arjun stared at her, struggling to find the right words, but none came. He had thought that once he came back from the glacier, things would fall into place. But now, sitting here, he realized how much he had taken her patience for granted.

"I don't want to lose you," he said softly, his voice barely audible over the hum of the café.

Zoya reached across the table, her hand covering his. Her touch was warm, but there was a finality in it that he couldn't ignore. "You're not losing me, Arjun. You'll always have a place in my heart. But I think we both know that we're not on the same path anymore."

Arjun swallowed hard, his throat tight with emotion. He wanted to argue, to tell her she was wrong, that they could make it work. But deep down, he knew she was right. He had always been restless, always searching for something more, and no matter how much he loved her, that part of him wasn't going to change.

"Maybe," she whispered, her voice breaking slightly, "maybe we've been holding on to something that's not there anymore."

The words hit him like a wave, and for the first time since they sat down, Arjun felt the reality of what was happening sink in. He had come back from the glacier thinking he could pick up where they left off, but the truth was, everything had changed. And not just because of what he had been through—because of who he was.

"I'm sorry," he said, his voice thick with emotion. "I never meant for it to be like this."

Zoya smiled through her tears, squeezing his hand one last time before letting go. "It's not your fault, Arjun. We just want different things now. And that's okay."

She stood up slowly, wiping away a tear as she did. "I'll always care about you, but I think it's time we both move on."

Arjun sat there, watching as she gathered her things, his heart aching with the finality of it all. He wanted to reach out, to stop her, but he knew there was nothing left to say. She was right—they were different now.

As Zoya walked toward the door, she glanced back at him one last time, her eyes filled with a mixture of love and sadness. "Take care of yourself, Arjun," she said softly before turning and stepping out into the cold.

Arjun sat in the café, staring at the empty seat across from him. The warmth of the coffee cup in his hands had faded, and the noise of the café slowly crept back into his awareness. He had survived the glacier, but now, sitting alone in the café, he realized that in his pursuit of something greater, he had lost something he could never get back.

The door jingled as someone else entered, but for Arjun, the world outside felt distant and foreign. He had always been chasing the next adventure, the next challenge. But now, he wondered if in doing so, he had left the most important part of himself behind.

Final Reflection

One evening, as Arjun walked home from the hospital, the roads of the cantonment seemed brighter than they had in a long time. The sun was setting, casting long, golden rays across the city, and the cool evening air carried a sense of calm that settled in his chest. For the first time since returning, he allowed himself to breathe deeply, to let go of the lingering weight of the glacier.

When he arrived at the house, his father was where he often found him—in the garden, sitting quietly in his favorite chair, a book open on his lap. Arjun paused at the gate for a moment, watching the man who had taught him so much about resilience and responsibility. His father hadn't asked many questions since his return, giving Arjun the space he needed, understanding that some battles couldn't be explained, only lived through.

Arjun walked over and sat down beside him on the weathered wooden bench. They didn't speak immediately; there was no need to. The comfortable silence stretched between them, as the birds flitted between the trees, and the distant hum of the cantonment life filled the air.

After a while, his father broke the quiet, his voice steady and thoughtful. "You look better," he said, glancing at Arjun out of the corner of his eye, but with a knowing smile that spoke volumes.

Arjun returned the smile, one that reached his eyes this time. "I feel better," he replied simply.

His father nodded, as if that was all he needed to hear. "Good," he said softly, his eyes returning to the horizon. "It's good to have you back."

They sat for a few more moments in silence, but it wasn't heavy like it had been in the past. This silence felt like healing, like the acknowledgment of battles fought and won—externally and internally.

The glacier, with all its cold and silence, had taught him something important: that survival wasn't just about making it through, but about coming out on the other side and willing to keep moving forward.

The shadows grew longer as the evening deepened, but as Arjun sat beside his father, watching the last of the sun disappear, he knew—he had survived, and now it was time to live.

www.ingramcontent.com/pod-product-compliance
Lightning Source LLC
Chambersburg PA
CBHW051235130726

47988CB00001B/358